JOSÉ VICENTE ALFARO

THE HOPE OF TIBET

First printed edition: March 2016

First digital edition: March 2016

© José Vicente Alfaro

Cover design: © Juan Luis Torres Pereira

Original Title: *La esperanza del Tíbet*

Translated from the Spanish by Christy Cox and Peter Gauld

Edited by Carmen Grau

For you, the reader. Thank you for sharing this adventure with me.

HISTORICAL TIBET

CHINA

KHAM

Wolong

Xiahe

Xining

Rushar

Monte Siguniang

Dartsedo

Monte Minya Gangkar

Gyeltang

Kanze

Litang

Batang

Dechen

Lago Kokonor

Monte Amne Machin

Derge

Jyekundo

Zagang

Baingda

Ponre

Metok

BIRMANIA

AMDO

Chamdo

Tengchen

Nyingtri

Tsetang

Golmud

Damrung

Lhasa

Lago Yandrok

Nakchu

Gurum

Gyantse

Monte Everest

Lago Namtso

Shigatse

BUTÁN

BANGLADÉS

CHINA

U-TSANG

Gyewa

Tsochen

Gertse

NEPAL

Rutok

Ali

Monte Kailash

Guge

INDIA

7

INTRODUCTION

According to Tibetan tradition, during the 7th century King Songtsen Gampo unified the different wild clans and the remotest fiefs of the Himalayas, finally making Tibet a tremendously strong nation. But not only did the mythical king bring peace and the creation of a written language; most specially, for the first time he introduced the Buddhism from India into the region.

Songtsen Gampo's successors continued his legacy, and during the following centuries established a large number of monasteries, which favoured the spreading of the way of the *dharma* far and wide across the so-called Land of the Snows. This process would culminate in the translation from Sanskrit into Tibetan of all the Buddhist texts. The movement attained such popularity that even the monastic institutions began to gain power, to the detriment of that of the governing noble families.

Tibet's particular orography, surrounded by immense mountain ranges, deserts, and lakes, all of which made access extremely difficult, gave the country natural protection from any foreign invasion until at the beginning of the 13th century the army of the mighty conqueror Genghis Khan stood at its borders.

In those days, the territorial superiority of the Mongol Empire made it the greatest known in the history of humankind. It reached from Poland to the Sea of Japan, and from the Siberian forests to the Persian Gulf. In the year 1207 Tibet was conquered without a single drop of blood being spilt, thanks to a pact under which the Tibetans had to pay tribute to the Mongols.

Nevertheless, on the death of Genghis Khan in the year 1227 the Tibetan governors stopped paying the tribute. As a consequence Prince Godan, the Great Khan's grandson, invaded Tibet in 1240, destroying and sacking all the monasteries, villages and hamlets in his way...

CHAPTER I

Equinox

"*As a mother, at the risk of her own life, watches over and protects her only child, so like a boundless spirit must we love all living things, love the whole world, above, below, around, without limits, with an infinite and benevolent kindness.*"

Suttanipata, 143 – 152

The Karmapa's life was waning. His time had come and he, more than anyone else, was perfectly aware of it.

The light of a bunch of candles penetrated the half-darkness of the room, showing glimpses of a beautiful fresco on the wall. It was dedicated to Avalokiteshvara, the most popular Buddhist deity among the Tibetans. Incense, burning as a symbol of purification, gave off an intense aroma which permeated every corner of the wide hall. The Karmapa was lying on his cotton bed, almost in his death throes, with a *mala* in his hands and a mantra in his mouth. He had the mala—the Tibetan rosary—wrapped around his wrist, and as he passed the beads he recited the tireless mantra of his own creation, the famous *Om mani padme hum*, barely moving his lips.

The old Buddhist leader awaited the moment of his death with a serene expression. The sunken eyes and faded cheeks were the only signs of the exhaustion of his worldly body. The Karmapa had served his people well. He had spent the first part of his life within the walls of the monastery, being trained in the ritual practices and religious services, learning the holy texts and meditating unceasingly. But the second part he had devoted to preaching the Buddha's teachings throughout Tibet as well as abroad, both to noble people and rulers and to the poor and disinherited of the land. The death of the old lama would not simply be one more death. The figure of the Karmapa as head of the Kagyu School, one of the most important in Tibetan Buddhism, was venerated by hundreds of thousands of followers due to his indisputable spiritual leadership.

Together with the Karmapa, accompanying him in his final moments, were two other lamas, both with shaven heads and the traditional saffron Buddhist tunic.

One of them, Tsultrim Trungpa, was looking out at the horizon through the window, below which lay the Tsurphu Monastery. It was set in the middle of a narrow valley at nearly fifteen thousand feet, near the town of Gurum and forty miles or so from Lhasa. Surrounded by high snow-capped peaks, it looked almost otherworldly. Tsurphu Gompa was the seat of the Karmapa. This true monastic city was a complex made up of temples, schools and residences, inhabited by almost a thousand Tibetan monks. Tsultrim stared out as far as he could. That morning the gompa was hidden by a thick white fog, a sure indication of the imminent death of the spiritual leader of the Kagyu lineage.

Tsultrim Trungpa was the abbot of Tsurphu Monastery. Thickly built and with eyes which bulged like those of a toad, he always appeared worried and nervous, a direct consequence of the burden of administrating a gompa such as this. He could only lighten this burden when he managed to lose himself in meditation or prayer. The abbot's thoughts were on the delicate political situation of the region. The Mongols had stopped their attacks some time before, but the news from beyond the borders told that two grandsons of Genghis Khan, Kublai and his brother Ariq Boke, had begun a war of succession to gain the title of Great Khan, and the effects the victory of either might have on Tibet were unpredictable.

The Karmapa interrupted his endless mantra to cough, and Tsultrim returned to his side by the bed. Kyentse Rinpoche was there. He had not left the old man for a single moment since the latter had announced his own death several days before, coinciding with the autumnal equinox. Kyentse was the Karmapa's foremost disciple. For the last fifteen years he had followed him in all his travels, absorbing his teachings and his wisdom. As time passed he had become not only his most faithful pupil but his personal assistant and secretary. In these troublesome moments a myriad memories were going round his mind. Kyentse had earned the honorific title of Rinpoche in acknowledgement of his advanced level of achievement and the high esteem in which he was held as a lama. Angular of feature, with closely set bushy eyebrows, the distinguished monk possessed great intelligence and unfailing reserves of energy. Kyentse Rinpoche bent over his master to ask if he wanted a sip of water to clear his throat, but the Karmapa refused and continued his prayers.

Tsultrim put his hand on Kyentse's shoulder and then, taking his arm, led him to the window. He only wanted to take him away from the Karmapa's bedside for a few minutes so that he could clear his mind.

"You should rest," said the abbot. "You have barely slept these last days."

"There will be time," replied Kyentse with a weak smile, "when the Karmapa is completely gone."

The fog vanished, allowing them to see the gompa's almost empty courtyards. The monks were gathered in the temples carrying out *pujas* in honour and worship amid chanting and bowing.

At that moment the Karmapa raised his arm feebly to attract the attention of the two lamas. Kyentse and Tsultrim went to him at once and stood one on each side of the bed. The Karmapa's eyes had turned glassy, he breathed with difficulty and his spirit was already struggling to leave his body for good. He took a deep breath to say his last words. Kyentse bent down over his master.

Finally, in a broken thread of a voice, the Karmapa said: "I am the one who seeks refuge in the refuge."

Next he continued with the mantra which had turned into a barely audible guttural sound—*Om mani padme hum*—and clasped his fingers over the *ghau* that hung on his chest. The ghau, a silver pendant with inlaid jewels, contained a tiny box of prayers which was used to hold the favorite mantra of its owner. The Karmapa loosened his hold on the mala in one hand, and the ghau in the other, then his voice faded away along with the brightness of his gaze. Moments later, after closing his eyes as though their lids weighed a ton, the Kagyu leader exhaled his last breath.

The funeral was held a few days later with all the pomp and magnificence the figure of the Karmapa deserved. A *stupa* was erected close to the monastery, inside which the ashes of the deceased were kept, together with other relics and consecrated objects. This traditional monument was considered the symbolic support of the spirits of the Buddhas. In future monks and laymen would walk around it in circles, always in a clockwise direction, following the path of the sun, to imbue themselves with his blessings and accumulate worthiness in the way of dharma.

After the funeral, the particular system of succession to guarantee the continuity of the lineage would begin, according to which it became necessary for the Karmapa's closest disciples to identify his new incarnation. For the great majority of Tibetans, rebirth was a certainty that affected everybody and admitted no argument. However, reincarnation was a different phenomenon and much more exceptional, exclusive to the great *bodhisattvas* who, given their high level of spiritual development, were able to consciously choose the circumstances of their future incarnation.

All this meant that a boy of special characteristics would appear in a few years. He would be the Karmapa reincarnated, known as a *tulku*, who would occupy the vacant position. In fact, a committee of wise monks would be designated, so that through their clairvoyance, intuition, visions and dreams, they would look for specific signs to lead them to the tulku's birthplace. Until then the Karmapa's rooms and belongings would be preserved intact, in a perfect state of conservation.

Kyentse Rinpoche and Tsultrim Trungpa maintained a conversation that was agreeable and trivial at first as they remembered the compassion and greatness of spirit of the late Karmapa, whom they had both loved. But then they turned to more serious and practical matters, acknowledging the threat that the absence of a visible head of the Kagyu School posed to Tibet in particular and the Buddhist world at large. The conflict with the Mongol empire required the help of all the Tibetan authorities, both political and religious, in order to procure the best possible destiny for their people.

They also discussed the last words the Karmapa had spoken just before he died. Neither of them could puzzle out their cryptic meaning. In a general sense, the phrase "take refuge" referred to a baptism of sorts, an allusion to the act of converting to Buddhism. But the Karmapa's sentence was as short as it was redundant, and equally incomprehensible to both.

"The sooner we find the tulku, the better," Kyentse declared.

"Let us trust," replied Tsultrim. "All the omens have been favorable so far."

* * *

Six years had passed since the death of the Karmapa. In the neighboring region of Kham, in the southeast of Tibet, a humble family of peasants was fleeing from the horror of the invaders. Although the Mongol sackings had officially stopped a long time before, the fact was that some military detachments posted in the remotest areas of the country, taking advantage of the impunity afforded them, on occasion turned a deaf ear to the orders of their superiors thousands of miles away and assaulted the farthest and least protected villages of their territory for the sheer fun of it.

The Norgay family fled with little more than the clothes they were wearing, leaving behind a life of hardship and toil. Urged on by the situation, they were forced to leave their home, their patch of arable land and their few animals in the blink of an eye. They threw the scarce belongings they were able to gather into a cart pulled by a yak, and without looking back they escaped from that place as if the devil were after them.

Jampo Norgay, the head of the family, had decided to travel toward Batang, a city which the Mongols would not attack and where he hoped to have a chance to start over from scratch. But the long journey was demanding a formidable effort: they had been traversing chasms and gorges along stony paths, made more dangerous by the heavy snowfalls brought on by the recent onset of winter.

They crossed the narrow, sinuous paths of a mountain pass which wound round the range. They had left behind dreamlike landscapes they could still easily see from their high position. The immense steppes alternated with red rock canyons and salty lakes whose waters reflected the pristine blue of a sky devoid of clouds. The swollen rivers flowed down furiously, bathing the shores and feeding the terraces where the cereals grew. In Tibet, the barrenness of fields full of stones and the infinite wealth of pasture-rich lands coexisted under the same relentless sun.

The Norgay family shared the traditional Tibetan features: wide faces, slanting eyes and high cheekbones. Jampo, weathered by the thankless tasks of the fields, was robust and vigorous. A man of few words and frugal in his show of affection, he was nonetheless devoted to making sure his family never lacked their daily sustenance, even though in order to obtain it he had to overload his back like a mule and steal hours of sleep before dawn.

Jampo walked beside the yak, patting the hump that emerged between his shoulders. Indeed, without the beast, the only animal they had been able to save in their hasty escape, they would never have been able to undertake an adventure like this. That male yak had helped him with the plough and was now pulling the cart that carried his family. He had thick heavy brown hair which protected him from the cold, long horns, and large hooves adapted to mountainous territory. The domesticated beast had not uttered a single complaint, even though they had not stopped once in their journey.

"Goddamn Mongols!" Jampo swore under his breath.

Settled in the cart, among their stuff, were Jampo's wife and his two small children. Dolma was thin as a stick but surprisingly strong, since she toiled in the fields with the same devotion and discipline as her hardworking husband. Despite this, Dolma kept a certain vanity, and was seldom seen without some kind of ornament – a bracelet or a pair of turquoise earrings – finished off by an unvarying central parting and two immaculate braids hanging on either side. The brave woman did not let the fear she felt inside show on her face so that the two boys would not realise how serious their situation was.

Thupten was six years old, Chögyam five. The older brother felt restless; as he was used to rushing round and not being still for a moment, the tedious imprisonment in the cart annoyed and bored him beyond measure. Thupten promised to be a tall ungainly young man, unless nature decided otherwise. He was already a head taller than his brother, and it seemed most likely that he would be taller than the average Tibetan. His vitality made him talk a blue streak, and it was not unusual for him to get on his father's nerves with his incessant questions and long monologues. His guileless smile and well-proportioned features barely served to conceal his ungraceful jug ears.

Chögyam, on the other hand, was the opposite of his brother: an incredibly calm boy, sensible and as laconic as his father. His straight fringe fell over his forehead and his enormous eyes lit up his face like lighthouses. It was striking that at only five he showed the same composure as an old man, or the patience of any adult.

Chögyam preferred to watch a flower opening in solitude rather than playing tag with other children among the bushes. He also showed signs of great intelligence, and at that stage it was already evident that it surpassed that of his older brother. Dolma even had an inward conviction that life held a different, more promising future for him than the one his birth had allotted to him.

Although the two brothers could not have been more different, they got along really well and there was great complicity between them.

"When will we go back home?" asked Thupten with a frown.

Jampo turned his head to Dolma and their eyes met in a despondent glance that would have made a plant wilt. Dolma remained silent and tried to smile while he thought which words to choose.

"We're never going back," said Chögyam.

Jampo and Dolma looked at each other again. It frightened them to hear a boy his age speak with such conviction.

"Is that true?" insisted Thupten, hoping more than ever that his younger brother was wrong.

"We shall be living in a new place now," replied Dolma. "We are going to the city. We hope to be as happy as we were in the village. Or perhaps even a little more."

On the horizon the snowy peaks were outlined in a sky spread with motionless clouds. Cliffs and crests of lesser height tore at a shroud of grey mist.

Dolma bent over a cloth bag to get some food that would satisfy their hunger and frighten away the uncertainties of the journey. She shared some *tsampa* with her sons, as Jampo refused the offer. Tsampa was the staple food of Tibet: roasted barley made into a paste and eaten with the fingers; it provided a substantial quantity of fat and protein. They ate in silence, used by now to the rattling of the cart, which jerked with every pothole in the road.

Jampo and Dolma had been united in their late teens. It had been an arranged marriage by their parents, although both of them liked to tell how love had germinated between them with the passing of time as a seed takes root in the soil. Dolma was from a distant village; her dowry had not been much, but Jampo's parents had accepted her and Dolma's family were able to get rid of one mouth to feed. Jampo's village lay at the foot of a mountain. The climate there was cruel and the earth so barren that it only produced one harvest of cereal a year, but hard work always bore fruit and in the end they managed to survive. During her two pregnancies Dolma had gone on with her tasks in the fields until the very same day of the birth and went back to work after a brief two-day rest. The couple felt blessed by having had two male offspring, who were so much more useful for farming than females and who had so far managed to survive an extremely high rate of infantile mortality.

Since the teachings of the Buddha had not reached their village yet, its religious needs were met by the celebration of ceremonies following a lunar calendar in which animals were sacrificed around a stone altar as offerings to nature and a series of ancestral gods. In winter, while the fields were left fallow, the peasants could at last enjoy a well-deserved rest and time for leisure. Social life became more active, and it was common for nearly all families to gather every day for a meal as if they were celebrating some festivity.

But now the Mongols had wrested everything from them.

"Mom!" Chögyam suddenly broke the silence. "Look! A lotus flower!"

"Here? Where?" Dolma asked in surprise. "They barely bloom at this time of year."

"There." Chögyam pointed at the mountain which ran parallel to the path they were following. "On that black rock."

Dolma strained her eyes and after a few seconds understood what her younger son was referring to. If you looked attentively at a jutting rock on the side of the mountain, it was possible to imagine the rough shape of a lotus flower, with spear-shaped concave petals in various layers, carved in profile on the rock itself and the folds of its relief.

"It's true!" Dolma acknowledged with a smile.

Jampo glanced at the whimsical natural formation but didn't pay it any more attention and went on walking beside the yak.

"I don't see it, Chögyam." Thupten whined. "Where is it?"

Chögyam pulled on his brother's sheepskin vest to make him stand beside him so that he could look at the mountain from the same angle. Thupten squinted his eyes and tried hard to see the shape the others could see so easily. When a minute later he succeeded, his face lit up, and he celebrated with cries of joy. "It's

he yelled. The echo of his voice rang in the depths of the
v valley.

Dolma congratulated Chögyam on his sharp sight and
feverish imagination. All three had finished their tsampa, and Dolma
began to prepare for what had become a ritual at dessert time. The
children could not have dessert after every meal, as any type of
sweet was a luxury in their circumstances. Because of this, Dolma
had invented a game for those occasions when she could make a
cake, in order to ration it as far as possible. She would hide a piece
in one hand, and each boy had to guess in turn which hand held the
treat. If they guessed correctly, they could eat the sweet right away;
if not, they had to save it for evening, after supper. At the same time
Dolma had the idea that by doing this she was teaching her children
a valuable lesson: that in life you cannot always have whatever you
want when you want it. What she did not know was that Thupten and
Chögyam had recently allied to always get away with it.

That day she had some cheesecake, called *tu*, made of yak
butter, brown sugar and water. The first turn was for Thupten, so he
stood in front of his mother. Dolma had cut a piece of the cake and
hidden it in one of her fists, with her hands behind her. She extended
her arms in front of her, fists closed, and encouraged Thupten to
guess which hand the treat was in. The brothers' secret lay in the fact
that meanwhile, Chögyam had stood beside his mother and seen
which hand she had hidden the sweet in. Thupten passed his fingers
over his mother's right hand, still without choosing, and glanced at
his brother out of the corner of his eye. Nothing happened. Then he
slid his fingers to the left hand and searched for the younger boy's
gaze again. This time Chögyam winked at him in a flash. The treat
was in the left hand, and Thupten pointed at it with absolute
conviction. Dolma opened her fist and there it was. The whole
operation was then repeated, although as Thupten did not know how
to wink, he blinked to give the signal.

In the end both brothers gobbled down their piece of cake,
while Dolma was becoming suspicious of the luck her children were
having of late.

Jampo, on his part, was worried. He had never been to
Batang and until now had been following the directions other
travelers had given him on the way. The problem was that they had
not come across anyone in a long time except for some goatherds

tending their flocks in the distance. What's more, the last person they had met before the mountain pass, a nomad who knew those lands well, had warned them that a fierce storm of snow and rain was approaching and had advised them to find shelter until it passed. But Jampo was so anxious to reach Batang, which lay round the hill, that he ignored the warning.

The path became narrow to the point there was barely room for the cart. On one side there was the cliff, a vertical wall a hundred and sixty-five feet tall, at the bottom of which was a cedar wood pearled with the white of first snow. On the other side there was the steep rocky side of the mountain, going up at a diagonal, rising above them with the insolence of the most ferocious nature.

Jampo kept the cart away from the edge of the path as much as possible, as a simple stumble could plunge them into the void.

"How long till we get there?" Thupten asked with visible displeasure.

Jampo bit his tongue so as not to let toads and snakes come out of his mouth. It was the umpteenth time Thupten had asked the same question, and he was beginning to get tired of it.

"Not long, my son," murmured Dolma. "You must be more patient."

Suddenly a gusty wind began to blow, the temperature dropped dramatically, and a freezing cold made its way into their bones. Chögyam was shivering like a tadpole but did not complain. Dolma put her arms round both her sons to provide some warmth and comfort.

A heavy rain, prelude to the predicted snow, came in over the mountain to complete a chaotic picture, heavy with danger. Jampo urged the yak to go more slowly, in an attempt to slow down the speed of the cart. The deluge was drenching them, and Dolma had nothing to cover the boys with. The rain beat on the ground, making a din which seemed to fill everything around them. The water struck the hillside violently, running down in rivulets along the ruts and cracks of the slope on to the path. The wind was beginning to whip round them ever more strongly.

Jampo was trying to soothe the yak so that he would take the path slowly but safely. He himself was trying to stay calm and face the situation with his senses alert. He knew the two boys were scared to death, and judging by Dolma's face so was she. Even Jampo himself lost heart when he heard a loud crack from the side of the mountain.

A rock the size of a head came loose and rolled downhill. It hit the path without touching them, bounced on the ground and rolled into the abyss on the opposite side.

Other rocks followed the first one.

Jampo acted at once, seeking safety for his family. He got closer to them and urged Dolma to get off the cart with the children. His voice was lost amid the roar of the rain and the howl of the wind, but Dolma understood and put the boys on the ground. Jampo led his wife and sons to the wall of the slope, as the only way to avoid the falling rocks was to flatten themselves against the side of the mountain as closely as possible.

Now the rocks were falling about them in an endless sequence. Luckily it did not turn into an avalanche, a disaster which would have doomed them.

A rock fell beside the yak, and Jampo decided to untie him from the cart and bring him with them as if he were another member of the family. He did not have time to even try: a huge boulder hit the cart and pushed it toward the abyss, dragging the beast with it. The yak felt the cart pulling and tried to fasten his hooves to the ground, but the surface was so slippery that the animal skidded and fell on his side, sliding slowly toward the precipice, dragged along by the cart. At that moment Jampo acted by instinct rather than reason. He thought he could still save the beast if he held onto it while Dolma untied it so that only the cart would fall. It was an extremely risky plan.

Jampo took a few steps and launched himself on the yak, seizing him by the horns.

"No, Jampo!" cried Dolma desperately. "Let him fall!"

The cart was already hanging over the cliff and the yak was also about to tumble. Jampo realized he could not support the weight of both. The poor animal was terrified and lowed desperately, his eyes reflecting his fear. Jampo's heart bled for him, but in the end he had to let him go. The yak slid a few more feet until he plunged into the abyss.

Thupten and Chögyam looked on in terror. The water had soaked them from head to toe, but that seemed to be the least of their worries.

"Come back!" Dolma yelled over the roar of the storm.

Jampo was at the edge of the precipice, watching everything he had been able to save before the Mongol attack disappear down the mountain. He could now say that he had nothing except for his pride and the warmth of his family. Such was his grief that for a few moments he did not notice the rocks, large and small, flying around him.

"Hurry up, Jampo!" Dolma insisted. "Come back to us!"

Jampo reacted at last and turned round, but by the time he realized it was coming a rock fell directly on him. He was unable to dodge it. It was not a very big one, but it hit him squarely in the chest, hard enough to make him lose his footing. He waved his arms to regain his balance, since he knew that otherwise he would go the way of the cart and the yak.

Dolma ran through the curtain of rain to help her husband. She stretched out her arm and tried to grab his hand but could only manage to touch the tips of his fingers. One more inch would have been enough to save him. Jampo lost his balance at last and knew instantly that he was falling to his death. Just before he disappeared down the gorge, Dolma saw incredulity in her husband's eyes as well as a shadow of guilt for not having been able to protect his family.

Dolma let out a harrowing scream and fell on her knees, her fists clenched in front of her body. Tears of pain, mixed with raindrops, ran down her cheeks and moistened her deepest soul. Thupten and Chögyam cried and sniffled, terrified by the tragedy they had just witnessed. It did not take Dolma long to realize this was not the best place to give herself over to lamenting. She had to go back to her children immediately. She stood up and started making her way back to the safety of the mountain slope.

She had not taken more than a couple of steps when she was surprised by a gust of wind which seemed more like a hurricane. The draught hit her so violently that it lifted her up and dropped her again like a rag doll.

In a way Dolma was lucky, because although she fell flat on the ground in the middle of the path, the wind could very well have thrown her straight to the bottom of the precipice. But her share of bad luck was heightened by the fact that the blow made her lose consciousness.

"Mom!" Thupten cried. "Get up!"

The boys noticed their mother was not moving, nor did she seem in a condition to do so. Besides, and worse still, the wind was gradually pushing her, making her roll on the ground, bringing her ever closer to the precipice. As frightened as they were, Thupten and Chögyam knew that unless they did something, Dolma was heading for the same fate as their father.

The two brothers looked at each other and without a word grabbed one another's hand and left the safety of the mountain that had until then protected them from the wind and the falling rocks. Once in the open, things intensified. The rain whipped at them and the wind made them stagger, so that they were compelled to lean against each other to keep their balance. It was an effort to move forward, with every step an epic conquest. Meanwhile they heard the whistling of the rocks detaching from the wall and barely missing them.

Dolma's body was on the verge of falling, but by now the boys had almost reached her. Thupten, being the older brother, let go of Chögyam's hand, took a step forward, and stretched to grab his mother's dress. His teeth were clenched and he was shaking. Then another powerful gust, in the form of a whirlwind, wreaked havoc again. Dolma was thrown toward the abyss like a sleeping angel descending to hell, borne by the hurricane winds. At the same time Thupten himself was pushed to the brink of the cliff, but he managed to grab the edge at the last minute. The six-year-old small child remained hanging in the void, knowing his hands would only hold him a few more seconds.

Although Chögyam had just witnessed his mother's death, he did not lose his nerve; Thupten needed his help, and he could still save him. Crawling in the rain, Chögyam reached his brother and even managed to grasp his arm... but he soon realised he did not have the strength to haul him up. The two brothers looked at each other for the last time, until Thupten could hold on no longer and his hands lost their grip.

Thupten began his descent into the void, when suddenly a gust of wind like the one before wrapped them up and turned the tables. Like an invisible hand, the wilful hurricane lifted Thupten up in the air and dropped him on the ground again, at the same time lifting Chögyam and throwing him down the cliff.

At that moment the storm stopped. The winds dropped, the rain vanished and as a consequence the rocks stopped tumbling down the slope onto the path. Thupten, looking out over the edge, watched the tree-filled ravine below which had now become his family's improvised graveyard. His eyes filled with tears as the sky began to weep in its own way, dusting the mountain with snowflakes.

What Thupten did not know was that unlike his parents, Chögyam had managed to save himself in a miraculous way. The flexible branches of a gigantic cedar had broken his fall, and the blanket of snow at the bottom of the valley had cushioned it. Chögyam had lost consciousness, but he was still alive.

For the moment.

CHAPTER II

Winter

"Just as fresh milk does not turn sour all of a sudden, neither do the fruits of bad actions arrive all of a sudden. Their malice remains hidden, like fire among the embers."

Dhammapada, 5-12

On the morning of the day when the Norgay family was to succumb to tragedy, the abbot of the Batang Monastery was returning to the city after several months of absence.

Lama Lobsang Geshe and the handful of monks who accompanied him crossed the doors of the enclosure they had missed so much after having visited multiple villages and hamlets tirelessly preaching the teachings of the Buddha. The other monks came at once to welcome them, inquire about their experiences, and learn the approximate number of souls the abbot had harvested for the good of dharma.

Lobsang's monastery was ruled by the principles of Theravada Buddhism, which felt itself to be closer than any other to ancient Buddhism. For this reason they tried to imitate the Buddha's behavior and that of his first disciples, who many centuries before had dedicated themselves to traveling through central India spreading the doctrine, without fixed abode, sleeping at a different shelter every night. The nomadic existence of the monks had turned sedentary over the course of time because it had to be interrupted during the rainy season, something which would lead to the building of the first monasteries. Lobsang was faithful to that premise of wandering Buddhism and did not hesitate to take to the road in order to make himself known, although the result of this was that he did not live for even half the year in the monastery he ruled.

All the members of the community welcomed him affectionately until it came to Dechen, who greeted the abbot with his usual coldness and vain air of self-sufficiency. It seemed that some things never changed. Resigned, Lobsang shook his head and watched Dechen move aside with the parsimony of a cat that has been ousted from its favorite spot. That grudging old man would never accept the fact that a lama from far away had taken over him as abbot.

Lobsang was indeed an exceptional lama who had been educated at the illustrious Tsurphu Monastery and whose dedication to his studies had allowed him to reach the level of *Geshe*. Nevertheless, once he had acquired the title, instead of continuing his career at Tsurphu as would have been expected, Lobsang shared with his superiors what his truest wish had always been: to lead a humble monastery in the Kahm region so that he could spread Buddhism throughout those remote villages, where it was still unknown. His decision was received with certain astonishment, for Lobsang might very well have been part of the Karmapa's inner circle and participated in important decisions. He could also have chosen a life of reclusion, as some others did, devoted to meditation on Mount Kailash or some other mountain near Lhasa. But no, Lobsang knew very clearly what his vocation was, and his superiors granted him the wish he had earned. His destination was the city of Batang, and his mission to assume the management of its small, languishing monastery.

It was ten years since then, and in spite of the time that had elapsed, Lama Dechen still refused to leave the past behind. The news of his replacement had upset him beyond measure, even knowing full well that Lobsang's level of Geshe fully equipped him for the post he himself had performed for innumerable years with more pain than glory. Dechen's first reaction was unworthy of a Buddhist monk, to the extent that he even refused to speak to Lobsang, as if the newcomer were responsible for what had happened. Later on he relented, reluctantly accepted his new status in the monastery, and even agreed to collaborate with Lobsang for the good of the community. That attitude, however, did not last long, and for a while now he had gone back to showing signs of his dissatisfaction. Dechen's only consolation was the new abbot's zeal for traveling, as thanks to that at least he automatically became his substitute during his prolonged absences.

The first time Lobsang arrived there, the monastery had looked ruinous and unkempt in equal measure. The prayer banners greeting the faithful at the entrance were nothing but dirty rags, and the weather had erased the holy words printed on them. The only stupa to grace the enclosure was literally falling to pieces and it was heartbreaking to walk around it as custom dictated. The frescoes were flaking off the outer walls at an alarming speed, obscuring the mandalas represented there for the delight of visitors.

Lobsang was immediately aware of the challenge involved in restoring the Batang Monastery to the place it deserved, but with effort and toil he succeeded.

At his arrival the community had consisted of thirty monks; the number now was over two hundred, and it was still growing. Lobsang had rebuilt the temple to make it three times bigger, had added new residences and even given it a library, something it had previously lacked.

Dorjee bowed to Lobsang and gave him a look that clearly revealed how much he had to tell him. Dorjee was a young monk whom Lobsang trusted completely to relate to him, reliably and in detail, everything that had happened in the monastery during his long absences. The responsibility should have been Lama Dechen's, but many years of experience had taught Lobsang that the substitute abbot restricted himself to replying with vagueness and scant interest, apart from the fact that Dechen himself was usually the cause of any conflicts arising in the monastery.

"Dorjee, come to my rooms in an hour to tell me all that's happened," Lobsang ordered. "But now, attend to the new novices who have accompanied me on my return journey."

Besides all those people Lobsang had succeeded in converting to Buddhism in the course of his preaching, there were also those who, captivated by the Buddha's teachings, showed a desire to join the monastic community of Batang. Some were young, some middle-aged; Lobsang made no distinction, although the older ones found it harder to integrate after years of secular life. Many belonged to the humblest level of society, but there were also those who, in spite of being rich and enjoying a privileged position, renounced their wealth with the intention of leading their lives in a deeper way. Others embraced monastic life after having suffered a trauma or some very painful experience, such as the loss of a child, and there were even those who did following in the steps of family or friends. The reasons for their joining were not important to monastic Buddhism; what really mattered was the way in which the renouncer led his religious life within the community.

Lama Dechen approached Lobsang to rebuke him for continuing to admit more members. "Very soon there won't be enough rooms for all," he said bluntly.

Lobsang could not believe Dechen had spoken to him solely in order to reproach him. He would have retorted that in that case they would have to build more, but Dechen turned his back on him and walked away quickly.

His hostile attitude was a clear sign on the horizon of the troubles that were to come.

Dorjee arrived punctually for his appointment with the abbot. The sight of Lobsang still impressed him, even though he had shared several years of living together with him. If it had not been for his dress, no one would have guessed Lobsang was a lama. His great height and robust complexion would have much better suited any other kind of work which required brute force. As a result of the austerity in their lives, monks in general didn't stand out for their athletic looks or battle-hardened air. Even so, the first impression Lobsang made on people with his mere presence would have been useless to him without his other basic weapon: an extraordinary charisma which immediately caught the attention of all those who attended his discourses. The warmth of his grave, deep voice, the intensity of his gaze, and the amazing ease with which he communicated fit like a glove with the level of knowledge he possessed due to his exceptional training.

Lobsang Geshe greeted the young monk leaning down his head and joining his hands together as though in prayer. Dorjee returned the greeting in the same way and with a warm smile. Lobsang's presence always filled him with a special emotion and a feeling of infinite gratitude. Dorjee had been trained at the Batang Monastery since he was a boy, coinciding with Lobsang's arrival and his installation as abbot. He had witnessed not only his inner growth but the growth of the monastery itself, which now could already be said to have the air of a small gompa.

"Dorjee, I beg you to tell me about all those matters whose delicate nature makes them unsuitable for common knowledge."

The young monk nodded and fixed his eyes on the ceiling, as if he did not know where to begin. "As you can imagine," he said at last, "Lama Dechen is the cause of most of the trouble. His attitude leaves much to be desired. In some cases he has relaxed the observance of the rules of monastic life, in others he has used subterfuges to avoid them, and in the remaining cases he has even flagrantly flouted them."

Monastic discipline was regulated by the Vinaya Pitaka. Some of its precepts originated in the Buddha himself, others were subsequently modified in commentaries, and the rest appeared at a later period. Whatever the case, the establishment of the rules was traditionally attributed to the Buddha himself, so that complying with them was considered supremely important.

"What rules has Dechen infringed?" Lobsang asked.

"To begin with, he doesn't respect the rule of fasting and eats as often as he feels like it," explained Dorjee. "The real problem is that a number of the monks see him and end up imitating his behavior. After all, Dechen represents the highest authority in the monastery when you're away."

The rules determined that monks and novices alike could eat only once a day and during a precise period of time which lasted from sunrise till noon, after which it was forbidden to take any kind of solid food, although it was permitted to drink fruit or plant juices. Despite being a harsh measure, there was a reason behind it. On the one hand it set out to avoid an excessive intake of food, which might be an obstacle to meditation and appropriate inner progress. On the other hand, it served a social function, for Theravada practice ruled that the monks could only obtain food by begging; that is to say that they could only provide for themselves from what lay society gave them when they went from door to door, armed with the shield of their faith and their inseparable bowl.

"Does he break his fast very often?"

"Nearly every day," said Dorjee.

A wave of indignation filled Lobsang's spirit. The defiant behavior of Lama Dechen sought more than anything to question his own authority and undermine his prestige as the head of the monastery. His resentment and frustration were so strong that they prevented him from realizing the negative effects of his acts, which could eventually affect the whole monastic community. Yet his lack of vision was apparently not enough to blind him to the fact that disobeying that rule was no more than a minor infraction, which did not involve any punishment other than confessing his fault before the group and showing true repentance.

"What else?"

"The *Uposatha* acts have been performed with extreme relaxation and without the appropriate rigor."

In its rules, the community allowed the celebration of different rites to guarantee the good development of the monastic order. The most important of these were Uposatha days, during which reflection and meditation were intensified, and in particular the disciplinary code was recited so that the monks could declare their errors.

"Sometimes not all the groups of rules were listed," Dorjee went on. "Or, for example, the attendance of the monks wasn't checked."

A deep sadness followed Lobsang's indignation. Dechen's resentment and his unbridled ego were driving him to act against the very essence of what Buddhism represented. Lobsang had to admit that the situation had escaped from his control. He should have solved this conflict with Dechen long ago and not allowed it to go so far. He had heard enough but let Dorjee go on telling him about what had happened.

"Another time, when a group of lay faithful were visiting the monastery, Lama Dechen placed a copper bowl filled with water on the floor and asked the visitors to put in it as many coins as they saw fit." Dorjee saw that Lobsang had put his hands to his head. "He claimed that by using this maneuver he was not violating the ban on touching money with his hands."

Lobsang was finding it ever harder to believe what he was hearing. Dechen had definitely crossed the line. In that particular case, concerning the rule established in the Vinaya texts, they both knew only too well that the rule which forbade the monks to touch money clearly referred to the act of accepting it, so that Dechen's argument did not have a leg to stand on.

"Thank you, Dorjee," murmured Lobsang. "That's enough. You may go back to your duties."

The young monk withdrew with a bow, leaving Lobsang deeply worried. Between the religious community and the lay society there was a relationship of complete symbiosis. The main duty of Buddhist monks was to watch over the spirituality of their people. Their righteous conduct was not only a matter of their own wellbeing, it also influenced the enlightenment and religious benefit of society as a whole. Moreover, the monks had to do everything possible to strengthen the faith of their followers and attend always to their spiritual needs. In exchange, the faithful lay followers provided the monks with everything they needed for subsistence: they supplied food and clothing and gave up land and materials for the building of the monasteries. The faithful were proud of their own generous attitude, since in this way not only did they contribute to the divine life but accumulated a balance of merit for their own future existence.

Was Dechen unaware of that delicate balance, and how it could be upset if either party failed to keep its end of the bargain? They, more than anyone else, had to set an example of trustworthy behavior based on the teachings of the Buddha; otherwise the people would be perfectly justified in reproaching them for their attitude and turning their backs on them.

Lobsang decided to wait until late evening to approach Dechen, thus giving himself time to calm down and deliberate about what to say to him.

He spent the rest of the morning in meetings, one after the other, with the monks responsible for the different areas of the monastery: the one in charge of rituals and services, the one in charge of furniture and clothing, the coordinator of studies, the librarian, the master of arts, and the one in charge of music and dance. All brought him up to date on their various tasks. The abbot set the tone and always had the last word on the functioning of the monastery, so Lobsang listened and then instructed them according to their demands and needs.

Around noon Lobsang received the visit of Tenzin, the rector of the Buddhist convent of the nuns belonging to the order of the *bhikkhuni*. Lobsang didn't receive her in his rooms but in the yard outside the monastery, as they walked in sight of other monks, since the rules forbade them to share a closed space with someone of the opposite sex.

Tenzin was a small woman, middle-aged like Lobsang, with a permanent smile and a look as transparent as the wind. Of her many good qualities, the most notable was her incredible will power. Tenzin's head was shaven like that of the monks, and she wore a habit of similar cut.

Firstly, Tenzin thanked Lobsang for the novices he had been able to bring to her order; they had been led that same morning to the convent she directed at the opposite end of the city. The monastery of the bhikkhuni had been created in accordance with Lobsang's advice, and his unconditional support had become essential for its opening and functioning. The abbot's wisdom had allowed them to organize themselves with the appropriate structure, and three years later they already boasted thirty devout nuns, having begun with just ten.

The happiness Tenzin felt at seeing Lobsang again could not eclipse the deep worry in her face.

"Tenzin, I can see your spirit isn't at peace. What's the matter?"

The nun did not reply at once. She was looking sideways at Lobsang as she walked at his side, breathing agitatedly. "It's about Lama Dechen," she admitted at last. "He's giving us serious trouble."

Dechen's name was coming up again, and not exactly in a complimentary context. Lobsang sighed and braced himself for the worst. He was reaching the limits of his patience.

"For weeks he hasn't respected the division of areas for collecting alms."

Bearing in mind that monks and nuns had to go out every morning to beg their daily food ration, the city had been divided into sectors which were then shared out between the monks and the nuns so as to prevent the same devout follower having to give twice.

"Could it have been a misunderstanding?" Lobsang asked with little conviction.

Tenzin shook her head. "I asked him to explain himself," she said, "but he doesn't even bother to answer. He simply ignores me and looks away as if I wasn't there."

"Dechen has lost all control," Lobsang admitted. "He honors neither his rank as lama nor his status as a wise man."

"But that's not all," Tenzin added. "We know that he's slandering us among the wealthier classes. He wants to disparage us with false accusations and allegations that we don't comply with the

Vinaya code, and that we're not worthy of living a religious life as men do."

Lobsang pondered about the matter in silence. The upper class of the city and the most prosperous families were sufficiently well-off to provide both for the monks' monastery and the bhikkhunis' convent. The origin of the conflict was not in the procuring of food; it was unfortunately rooted in the implacable male chauvinism which had belittled women since time immemorial, reducing their role to that of mere puppets, always subject to man's will and his violent nature. Dechen had never liked the idea of the bhikkhuni order founding a convent in Batang, but until he openly declared war on Lobsang, who had supported the project from the beginning, he had not made the decision to campaign against the Buddhist nuns. Dechen seemed to want to forget the Buddha's revolutionary affirmation that women and men alike could reach enlightenment. Buddhism had placed women on an equal plane to men, in clear distinction to what was happening in all the world's other main religions. Another thing was the heavy load that society continued to drag in the form of historical male chauvinism, something which was very difficult to get rid of, or even get under control.

"We fear Dechen's slanders might end up affecting the population. If that should happen, we'd be left to our fate, or maybe something even worse."

Lobsang stopped short and fixed his gaze on Tenzin's eyes. "That will never happen as long as I'm abbot."

"Thank you," murmured Tenzin recovering her usual cheerful expression.

"As for the matter of alms, now that it's winter, it won't be a problem."

The harshness of the climate in winter freed the monks from their duty to gather alms until mid-spring. Therefore, it was the only time of the year when they were allowed to store food in the monastery, to be cooked and shared out diligently.

"Regarding the second matter," said Lobsang, "leave that to me. I have many things to discuss with Dechen."

After devoting some time to seclusion and tending to other duties required by his position, Lobsang summoned Dechen in the early evening. Through the window, as he waited, he watched the rarified sky above the mountain pass which gave access to Batang from the west. He hoped no one would be irrational enough to dare cross the paths that wound round the range at that time, since a heavy storm was approaching which would pose a serious threat to any traveler.

The sound of a cough behind him made him turn. Lama Dechen was planted there, slightly bent, looking at him with absolute indifference. Dechen was thinly built and with many years behind him, as shown by the endless wrinkles that, like the pattern of threads in a tapestry, made up his gaunt, rat-like face. A deep egocentrism and an entrenched bitterness had bent the simple spirit of a lama who, without being exceptional, had carried out his obligations honorably until Lobsang's arrival brought out the worst in him.

The hours Lobsang had let pass before the meeting now enabled him to face the interview calmly enough to avoid losing his temper with Dechen.

"I have already been informed of your behavior during my absence: the permissiveness you have allowed in following the rules, your own slackness in your duties, and even the faults you yourself have had no hesitation in committing. I'm surprised you've gone this far, Dechen. Your behavior is unacceptable, and you more than anyone else must be aware of that. What do you intend by all this? Do you want to create a rift among the monks of the community? Lose the respect of our faithful? Or do you think one day I'll grow so tired that I'll decide to leave this place?"

"Does it matter? You're the abbot of this monastery, but you don't spend even half the year in it." Dechen's attitude was more than defiant, it was cunning, like a fox's.

"Have you forgotten that our duty is to preach the doctrine? How will we do it if we don't lead our people along the way of dharma?

"Send others to do it in your stead."

Lobsang did not wish to argue and was not prepared to let himself be trapped by Dechen's provocations. The purpose of this meeting was as a warning, and nothing more. Lobsang had all winter ahead to put the old lama in his place.

"I want you to know something else," Lobsang said raising his voice. "Of all your reproachful acts, the worst is your petty attack on the honor of Tenzin and the Buddhist nuns."

"Religion isn't women's natural setting," Dechen replied. "And I'm not the only one who thinks so."

"You're more of a fool than I thought you were," Lobsang said. "The bhikkhuni contribute as much as we do, if not more, to elevate the spirituality of the population. They give themselves fervently to meditation, and their prayers have the same effect as ours."

This time it was Dechen who evaded the argument. He simply snorted and showed his impatience by drumming gently on the floor with the sole of his foot.

"Listen to me carefully," Lobsang said sternly. "You shall confess each and every one of your faults in the next Uposatha and express sincere repentance. Is that clear?"

Dechen did not have the nerve to hold Lobsang's gaze more than a few seconds. He mumbled something and went back where he had come from, harboring a little more hate in the depths of his soul.

Then the room once again regained the sound of silence and the harmony of a balanced karma.

Lobsang went to the window and looked up at the sky. The focus of the storm had moved from the peak of the mountain, leaving behind a group of clouds in the shape of a spiral which was shedding an avalanche of snowflakes.

* * *

Thupten came away from the edge of the precipice that had taken his family's lives, unaware that his younger brother had survived the fall and was breathing softly in the bowl of the valley, buried in a pile of snow and frost.

When he raised his eyes to the summit of the mountain, he saw a group of clouds in the shape of a spiral spewing out snowflakes that came down around him. Thupten was shivering with cold, but even more because of the tragic loneliness he found himself in all of a sudden. Like an automaton, trying not to think so as not to give in to the fear that was creeping along his skin like a poisonous snake, Thupten began to walk in the direction they had been heading in when they were surprised by the storm.

His teeth were chattering uncontrollably and his legs shaking as if he had lost control of his limbs. He walked hunched, with his arms wrapped around his middle, seeking the shelter of his own embrace and the little warmth his body gave off. Thupten walked along the mountain path in a stupor, eyes half-closed and gaze fixed on the ground, which was beginning to vanish under the falling snow. As he walked on, the dim daylight gave out completely and night slid in silently, accompanied only by the whistling of the wind zig-zagging among the peaks of the mountain range.

Hours might have gone by, or only minutes; Thupten could not tell. But when he raised his head again, he saw the outline of a city at the foot of the mountain, suspended in the darkness and wrapped in a shroud of suspicion. The path took a sudden abrupt downward turn that led directly to the heart of Batang.

For someone whose only point of reference had been a tiny hamlet, the city was a source of confusion, mixed with a strong element of wonder, even though at that moment Thupten could only think that reaching Batang was no more than the first step in saving his life, without stopping to consider anything else.

The stone and mud houses were pressed tightly against each other as if space were a fundamental factor there. The flat rooftops accumulated up to fifteen inches of snow, which would have to be shoveled off the next morning. The streets were narrow, and there was no one to be seen wandering along them. Darkness drowned the place with its disturbing presence. The cold, the night, and the accursed storm had confined people behind the walls of their homes; the boy could make out the gleams of their fireplaces through the windows.

Thupten glimpsed a couple of pedestrians slipping down the street like elusive ghosts, but before he could even get close to them, he lost them around a corner or behind some door. He felt his body freezing, with hunger added to his list of woes, so he had no choice but to go to one of the houses at random and knock on the door in the hope of being lucky.

He was about to do that when a man approached him in the street and showed an interest in him. "Hey, boy, how come you're not at home?" His voice was hoarse, and the tone he used did not sound totally sincere, but darkness masked the man's face and Thupten was unable to guess his features or read his look.

"I have no home," he whispered. "My family died in the mountain and I'm all alone." As soon as he uttered those words, Thupten broke down in a gush of sobs. The pressure of the terrible situation which had befallen him was a lot more than a six-year-old boy could bear.

"Calm down, son. I'll take care of you," said the man. "What's your name?"

"Thupten, sir," the boy said, holding back his sobs.

"My name is Wangchuk. And now that we know each other, you'd better come home with me."

Wangchuk turned around and began to walk away without checking whether Thupten was following him or not. There was something in the man which in spite of his apparent kindness made the boy a little distrustful. Nevertheless, Thupten felt he had no alternative, and given the circumstances it would be foolish to refuse the help he was being offered.

Wangchuk turned into a long street, walking very fast. Thupten tailed behind him, staring enviously at the thick yak fur the man wore wrapped around him like a cloak for protection against the low temperatures. They went through deserted streets and circumvented the city without Wangchuk stopping at any residence. Any one of them would have been enough for Thupten, even the humblest, as long as he could warm himself, eat something, and if possible sleep until the next day and wake up to find that it all had been nothing but a horrible nightmare. They soon reached the southern limit of the city, but Wangchuk did not slow down in the least. They left Batang behind, and the mysterious man went on up a long rise without a word. Every once in a while he would look out of the corner of his eye to see that the boy was following faithfully and had not had second thoughts about his offer. As the city lost itself in the night, Thupten's mistrust grew with every step.

"Where are we going?" he asked at last, afraid of sounding ungrateful to the man who had offered to help him.

"Don't fret, son. My house is on the outskirts. You'll see how you like it."

The reply did not comfort him in the least, but he knew that by then there was no going back. Besides, he was running out of strength, so much so that he had already resolved to give in to the supposed benevolence of this Wangchuk.

At last, in the middle of nowhere, a tiny wood cabin appeared on the horizon at the top of a hillock on the plain.

The outside of the hut was pitiful, but at least he had to admit it was a shelter. Wangchuk opened the door and invited Thupten to go inside. As soon as he did, a strong stink reached his nostrils, making him gag. There was a pile of sacks of dried yak manure in a corner; Tibetans used it commonly as fuel. Besides the manure he could only make out some wooden planks on the ground and a mess of dried leaves which must have been used as a mattress. Thupten would have burst into tears if he had had less courage and shame.

Wangchuk quickly made a fire with the yak manure. The fire lit up the place and gave Thupten the caressing warmth without which he would have ended up dead from hypothermia. By the light of the flames Thupten was able to take a good look at Wangchuk for the first time. The man was dressed in rags under his precious yak fur, his skin and nails were dirty, and behind his false smile was an irregular row of yellowed teeth.

Wangchuk took a piece of shriveled meat from a board and began to cook it over the fire.

"I'm hungry," Thupten whispered.

Wangchuk did not bother to pretend any longer, and his attitude toward Thupten took a radical turn. "This is only for me," he said. "Starting today, if you want food you'll have to earn it."

Thupten perceived Wangchuk's fetid breath in spite of the heavy atmosphere. He also realized something he had not noticed before: instead of his left hand, Wangchuk had only a repulsive stump.

"Just a little piece, please," Thupten begged, glassy-eyed.

Wangchuk moved like lightning, grabbed the boy's hair, and drew him close with such violence that he almost pulled out a lock of his hair. "Don't be ungrateful, boy. I've given you shelter when you had nothing. If you ever answer back at me I'll beat you up, and I won't stop until I break every bone in your body."

Silence returned to the cabin, interrupted only by the crackling of the fire and Thuptsen's sobs.

Before becoming an outlaw Wangchuk had been a shepherd. In fact his good knowledge of the region had led him to discover the cabin where he took shelter, which he knew was deserted during the winter months. Wangchuk's personal descent into hell had its origin in his love for alcohol. When he began to drink in excess, the cattle he used to take out to graze between the plains and the mountain sides started to wander off. At first he would lose one or two goats at every outing, and because of his inebriation he would be unable to find them again. In the end, after a drunken spree which left him unconscious, he lost the whole herd and with it his way of making a living.

Another bad decision made his situation even worse. While drunk, he had the idea of stealing something valuable to trade for some money. He was caught at once and was consequently given a severe punishment as a thief. Tibetan law was very clear on the subject: Wangchuk had his left hand firmly tied until the blood circulation stopped, then it was cut off with one stroke, and next the stump was dipped in a pot of boiling oil in order to cauterize the wound. From that day on Wangchuk had been an outlaw, left to his own fate.

Thupten's belly was growling so loudly that he dared to beg for a piece again. If he had known Wangchuk better he would not even have thought of it, but it was too late to retreat. The outlaw lunged at Thupten in a fit of rage, lifted him with his remaining hand, and threw him into a corner. The boy hit his side on the ground and watched in terror as Wangchuk, still not satisfied, came at him with eyes full of fury and feet aiming at his stomach. The kicks came from all sides, and Thupten rolled himself into a ball trying to minimize the impact of the ones on his ribs.

"And if you try to escape, I swear I'll cut you into little pieces!"

Wangchuk sat down beside the fire again, somewhat calmer after the lesson of discipline he had just given the boy. Shortly afterward he put out the fire, leaving just the embers to warm them during the night.

Thupten, sore and scared to death, did not move from the corner where he had been beaten. Nor was he able to sleep a wink all night.

The next day they got up early and immediately began the long, tiresome walk that separated them from the city. A cloak of snow over the plain prevented them from seeing the paths, but that did not bother Wangchuk, since he knew those lands like the palm of his hand. The outlaw behaved naturally, as if he had not mercilessly attacked Thupten the night before. He barely spoke to him during the way and when he did he used a neutral, distant tone of voice. "Today you'll earn your keep and show me what you're worth."

Thupten was so hungry that he was willing to do anything as long as it would feed him.

They reached the city and went through what looked to the boy like the poorest neighborhood. A woman who had no way to boil water put it in her mouth to warm it, then spit it out over her baby and licked him clean with her own tongue. The streets had come alive, looking very different from the night before. They walked among the crowd of people, who, deep in their own affairs, barely noticed their presence. Thupten saw that Wangchuk was covering part of his face with his coat and never allowed his left stump to be visible.

They reached their destination at last. The outlaw hid with Thupten at his side in the inside a side street with no traffic, from which they had a clear view of the food market. There were not so many stands at that time of year, but there were still enough to make Thupten's mouth begin to water. Many of the stands offered meat, cheese, and yak lard.

"Listen to me carefully," Wangchuk said, waving his finger in front of the boy's face and handing him a small cloth bag. "Follow my instruction to the letter and everything will be all right. See that stall with all the berries?"

Thupten nodded. The Tibetan berries of the Goji bush grew in the Himalayan valleys. Bright red, the size and texture of a raisin, they had a sweet taste similar to cherries.

"Good, then while I entertain the vendor, you come up from the other side and without anybody noticing, fill the bag as fast as you can."

"I have to… steal?" whispered Thupten.

"Would you rather starve?"

Thupten knew stealing was wrong, but he was unaware of the terrible consequences if he were caught doing it. Wangchuk purposefully omitted that part so as not to scare the boy further and to count on his complicity.

"You go first, then I will. It's important that we're not seen with each other, so that nobody will associate it us. If anything unplanned happens, don't let them catch you, and try to hide here."

As the boy was not moving, Wangchuk gave him a push to start him off. He was nervous from head to toe, so that until the moment of truth arrived not even Thupten himself knew whether he would be capable of carrying out the intended robbery. Still, the boy walked toward the market, staring at the exquisite delicacies laid out on the stands. Since he was a small child, he passed unnoticed among the bustle of the bazaar. The customers examined the quality of the products, while the vendors proclaimed loudly the excellence of their goods. Thupten waited for what seemed an eternity, until he saw Wangchuk approach the berry stall and pretend an interest in the tasty fruits worthy of the greatest expert.

Thupten stood at the farthest corner of the stand and prepared the bag to store the loot in. For his part Wangchuk had managed to ensure that the vendor was standing with his back to the boy. It was now or never. Thupten stretched out his hand, grabbed a bunch of berries and put them in the bag. Then he looked around, his face contorted with nerves. It seemed nobody had seen him. The impunity of the theft increased his confidence, and he repeated the process several more times. It was his fierce hunger which led him to make a mistake. He was unable to wait until he had finished his task and took a mouthful of berries, whose sweet smell had been making his mouth water and whose beauty had seduced him. The vendor, who every once in a while scanned his surroundings, did not see him steal, but caught him chewing with delight: enough to raise his suspicions. Seconds later, after watching him out of the corner of his eye, he surprised Thupten red-handed.

The vendor cried out and moved round the stand to grab the pilferer. Thupten was startled at being caught out and became paralyzed for a moment. Wangchuk then intervened. Apparently by accident, he tripped the vendor as he passed beside him, and then blocked his way as he apologized repeatedly for the unfortunate incident. The few seconds Wangchuk had gained gave Thupten time to escape into the crowd and out of danger.

Thupten considered the possibility of escaping from Wangchuk as well, but he discarded the idea. On the one hand he was still under the effect of the fear the outlaw had instilled in him the night before, convinced that if he failed in his attempt, Wangchuk would cut him into a thousand pieces. On the other hand, he had nowhere else to go and no one else to trust, particularly now that he was a thief and anybody could give him away.

So, after a while Thupten went back to the alley, where Wangchuk was already waiting for him. The outlaw was furious. His bloodshot eyes made the boy fear the worst, but luckily his rage did not go any further than that. Wangchuk took his share of the blame in the failed mission for not having prepared the boy well enough.

"We'll have to go back to the cabin," he said. "We shouldn't be seen in town today."

Thupten had mixed feelings. The relief he felt at not having to rob again, even if it were only for that day, contrasted with the anxiety of knowing he had another day ahead of him without food.

On the way back, as they were leaving the outskirts of the city, a street dog came to Thupten and sniffed him, looking for food. The mutt, with abundant hair and very lively eyes, was wagging his tail excitedly. Thupten could give him nothing but a little affection. He patted him, and that must have satisfied the dog enough to make him decide to follow the boy from then on.

They left Batang behind, but that did not discourage the dog in his determination to follow Thupten. Once again the only company they enjoyed was that of nature itself in the form of some trees in the distance and the snow-covered fields. Thupten stopped at times to play with the dog, until he noticed the reproving look of the outlaw, whose hostility made him move on briskly. Thupten daydreamed: if Wangchuk allowed him to keep the animal, his company, the hours of entertainment, and his affection would be enough to comfort him.

Thupten kept playing with the dog as he thought about, thinking what name to give him.

Halfway there, Wangchuk bent over to pick up a rock the size of his fist and waited for Thupten to catch up with him. Neither the expression on his face nor his gestures betrayed what he intended to do. Thupten, who would never have imagined it, did not even see it coming, but the dog did and by a hair's breadth managed to dodge the brutal blow aimed at its head. The rock brushed the back of the animal at the same time as the horrified boy understood the outlaw's intentions. Wangchuk cursed through his teeth and, carried on by the inertia of the failed blow, lost his balance and fell flat on his face. Thupten wished with all his heart that the dog would take that opportunity to run away from Wangchuk's cruelty. And he nearly managed to. However, the outlaw grabbed one of his legs just as he was beginning to run.

The dog turned on him and tried to bite him, but Wangchuk recovered quickly and threw himself on the animal in a one-to-one fight in which he had the advantage of size. The outlaw used his one hand to hold the dog's jaws shut and the weight of his body to immobilize him. The dog twisted, growled, and yelped pitifully, the sounds making their way through his throat and vanishing into thin air when they passed his teeth.

"Thupten! Don't just stand there!" Wangchuk shouted. "Take the rock and crush the damned dog's skull!"

The boy did not immediately react. He had been forced to steal for Wangchuk, but what he was asking now was too much.

"Do it now, or I swear you'll regret it!" cried Wangchuk, who was struggling furiously with the animal.

Panic took control over Thupten making his mind believe that he was not responsible for his actions. He took the rock with both hands and delivered the blow with all the strength he was capable of. The blow broke Thupten's heart, but not the dog's skull. He went on howling with pain and struggling to free himself from Wangchuk's grasp.

"Again!" bellowed the outlaw.

Thupten closed his eyes and began to deliver blow after blow. Blood spattered onto his face and mixed with his own tears, which rolled down his cheeks. When he dared to look again, he had split open the poor animal's head, leaving the brains exposed and pools of blood all over the ground. Thupten then collapsed and wept inconsolably, like the little boy he was.

Wangchuk stood up and hauled the dog over his shoulder. "Let's go," he ordered. "We have food for several days with this. You've earned it."

Wangchuk thought he would make more use of Thupten if he set him some task other than stealing, for which he didn't seem to be a natural and which was in any case too risky for him to assume at such an early age. From then on, the outlaw made the boy beg in the streets of Batang, always in his sight from somewhere nearby.

For Thupten this was the worst possible sentence. He had always driven his mother crazy back at their hamlet and made everyone dizzy running here and there, never still in one place.

"And look sad!" Wangchuk said over and over.

At first Thupten replied he would not need to fake because that was how he felt. There was no ulterior motive in his reply, nor did he mean to defy Wangchuk: both Thupten's garrulity and his obvious intensity were part of his nature. Yet he gradually learned to bite his tongue, as Wangchuk never took his replies well and was in the habit of twisting his ears, which, as they already stuck out from his head, caught his attention easily.

As the days passed Thupten's personality, subdued by the circumstances, turned reserved and taciturn in self-defense. He didn't obtain much from begging, but it was just enough to get by. In all likelihood, the sight of a boy with no disabilities or apparent problems did not awake compassion in the passers-by.

"Be thankful I don't take your eyes out or cut off a leg," Wangchuk said every once in a while. "Blind or lame you'd be more useful."

Wangchuk began to drink again, using part of what Thupten gained through begging. Although that meant less food for Thupten, it also had a positive effect: when the outlaw was drunk he forgot about him to some extent and was not so prone to hit him for a misplaced comment or what he considered an impertinent look.

One night, when Wangchuk was sleeping soundly after one of his usual binges, Thupten gathered enough courage to make an attempt at escaping in the dark, since by now he knew the way to the city by heart. He did not even get to the doorway. As if he had a sixth sense, the outlaw opened one eye in his sleep and surprised Thupten tiptoeing toward the exit.

Wangchuk had sworn to tear the boy to pieces if he ever tried to leave his side. In the end he did not keep his promise, but he gave him such a beating that he broke several of his bones and crushed his spirit for good. Thupten remained in the cabin, unable to move for fifteen days in a row. Wangchuk sent him begging in the streets of Batang as soon as he was able to stand straight and take a few steps.

Thupten did not believe he would survive a winter which seemed never-ending to him; he would succumb to the cold, malnutrition, and the outlaw's beatings. He wished that the miraculous draught of wind that had saved him at the last moment from falling to the abyss had never appeared. Then he would be dead, and his brother Chögyam would still be alive.

* * *

Chögyam opened his eyes, blinked several times, and looked around, feeling utterly confused. The dimness of the place contributed even more to his bewilderment. A long silhouette, like a faceless shadow, leaned over him.

"Are you all right?"

Chögyam's eyes began to adjust to the twilight of the place and at last managed to make out the features of the man who was watching him intently.

"Yes, sir."

He was an old man; Chögyam would have guessed him to be a thousand years old. His pitiful presence was reduced to little more than a skeleton covered with grayish, almost green wizened skin and two eyes that had lost any trace of color. A web of dirty, tangled hair fell to his shoulders and a full, thick beard hung down to his waist.

"Where am I?" asked Chögyam.

48

"This is my shelter," the old man said. "A cave in the mountain." His voice was surprisingly mild and soft, contrasting deeply with his ruinous appearance.

Chögyam sat up and stared at everything curiously. The place was no more than a cramped hole, so much so that the old man had to crouch to get inside. The stone floor was rough and irregular and the walls damp and rugged. This unusual dwelling lacked any kind of furniture. The cave was at best a tiny bite in the rock of the mountain.

The memory of the terrible events on the path at the mountain pass came back suddenly to Chögyam's mind. First he was overcome by a deep feeling of sadness, then one of fear and helplessness. Following an impulse, he decided to take a few steps and get out of the cave; the old man said nothing and simply watched.

Outside, everything was covered with snow. Chögyam saw that the cave was about halfway along a steep footpath up the mountainside. At the bottom of the valley was the forest of giant cedar trees whose leaves had saved his life, while above his head was a sparsely grown slope, splashed with rocky outcrops covered in moss and schist. Not too far above the cave a brook had run, now frozen. From that high place, the amazing panorama was of a vast range whose peaks were covered with a white blanket of snow.

Chögyam noticed at once the profound silence reigning in that landscape, not broken even by the singing of birds or the murmur of a river, and disturbed only by the roar of the winds between the chasms. The cold outside was extreme, and in comparison the warmth of the grotto, given its natural conditions, provided a certain relief. Chögyam focused his thoughts on his older brother. He thought Thupten must still be alive somewhere, and with that idea in mind he went back into the hollow.

"Will you take me to the city?" he asked the old man.

"I couldn't do it even if I wanted to," the old man replied. "In the winter this narrow, nameless valley is completely cut off by an impenetrable barrier of ice and snow."

Chögyam lowered his gaze to the ground tearfully.

"You'll have to wait until someone comes for you," the old man added.

The boy seemed to ponder that statement for a few seconds. Then he said, "How could anyone come for me if no one, except perhaps my brother, knows I'm here?"

"Earlier, while I was meditating and in a deep trance, I had a clear vision," the old man explained. "Avalokiteshvara himself, the personification of compassion and infinite love, appeared to me to tell me I should go to the bottom of the valley to rescue you from certain death by hypothermia. He also said I should instruct you and care for your wellbeing. And lastly, he revealed to me that a few people will come here to claim you. Apparently you're a very special child."

Chögyam was making an effort not to cry, although he could not help a few tears running down his cheeks.

"During the time we're together I'll teach you the dharma." The old man saw the uncertainty in the boy's face. "The dharma is the Buddhist path," he explained. "Haven't you ever heard of the Buddha?"

Chögyam shook his head.

"Well, in that case I'll enlighten you."

The old ascetic, who had spent the last forty years in absolute isolation in the mountain cave, was a revered lama educated at the Samye Monastery, the oldest in all Tibet. At the age of thirty-five he had solemnly vowed to meditate without interruption in a distant place until he attained Awakening. The brave lama had decided to reach Enlightenment in a single life, when the great sages held that to manage it in three lives was a great feat in itself. Most ascetics would seek refuge in one of the many caverns on the holy mount of Kailash, whose retreats attracted the pilgrims that wished to receive the blessings of those holy men. That was why the lama from Samye, more determined still, had opted to retreat to a forgotten mountain in the region of Kham. Chögyam was the first person he had had contact with since the beginning of his spiritual retreat, four decades earlier.

"What's your name?" he asked.

Chögyam whispered his name, holding back his tears.

"Well, my first lesson will be that you shall never again spend your time crying."

Chögyam nodded, sniffed back his tears and wiped his face with his fists. Then he said, "What is your name?"

The hermit, in his renunciation of desire and attachment to material things, and centered on his obstinate quest to span with his mind the true reality of the universe, had renounced even his own identity.

"I no longer have a name," he replied, "so from now on you'll have to call me 'master.'"

Chögyam nodded and instinctively bowed. He did not shed a single tear again in the presence of the old man.

Chögyam soon found out for himself how hard life could be in the cave, particularly in winter.

The business of food was by far the most traumatic. The hermit's diet was limited to the leaves of plants or roots he unearthed; no doubt, Chögyam thought, that was why his skin had taken on that olive-green tone that gave you such a shock when you first saw him. He was even more impressed to learn that during some stages of his retreat the old man had fasted completely for short periods, and at other times he had lived only on nettles. So Chögyam had no choice but to get used to eating what he had always considered food for goats. At least water was not a problem, thanks to a natural spring nearby, although in winter the water stopped running because it solidified like an ice floe, but then they got water from melting snow: a slow, tedious process which exasperated Chögyam.

At night, the little boy curled into a ball and tried to sleep on the damp stony floor, where there was no way of getting comfortable without feeling a bump on one side or the other, or in his back. More striking still was the fact that the hermit scarcely slept at all, since he considered it a waste of time. The hermit lama practiced the sophisticated techniques of the legendary sages and could alter his consciousness during meditation so that his organism rested.

The freezing winter temperatures did not make it advisable to go out. Chögyam only left the cave to relieve himself, and the first time he saw his urine turn into an icicle he hardly knew whether to laugh or cry. On those occasions he would see some large feline tracks on the snow, with a hole in the middle, which the old man attributed to the mythical snow leopard. He had only caught glimpses of it a couple of times during his prolonged stay in the mountains, and in spite of its reputation as a fierce predator it had never caused him any trouble.

At sunset, the cold turned unbearable even inside the cave, and Chögyam's sheepskin vest was not enough to keep him warm. On the third night he told the hermit, who without hesitation gave him his thin cotton cloak. Chögyam felt terribly guilty for having stripped the old man of the only garment he possessed; seeing him so unprotected he decided to return the cloak, because he thought that if he did not the old man would freeze during the night.

"Don't you worry about me." The hermit refused to take it back. "I don't need it."

"Are you sure, master?"

The lama, who was meditating in the lotus position, told Chögyam to touch his arm for one second and he would understand. The boy did what he was told by stretching his hand toward the old man's body. Even before he touched him he felt an intense heat which made his jaw drop. And when he touched his skin, it felt so hot it nearly burned his fingers.

The hermit told Chögyam about *tummo*, the mystical heat which Tibetan yogis and sages had learned to invoke and which made them immune to low temperatures. Chögyam listened, absorbed, and watched him with his immense brown eyes through his fringe.

"Could I practice tummo as well?"

"It's too soon yet. First I must teach you to meditate, but in time I'm sure you'll master it."

Shortly after Chögyam composed himself to sleep, but even with his master's garment could he alleviate the cold. So without a second thought, and once he was sure his master was in one of his introspective trances, he climbed onto his lap and fell asleep instantly. That routine would be repeated night after night.

After all the trouble the hermit had taken to isolate himself from the world and avoid contact with any human being with the goal of giving himself to tantric and meditative exercises in order to reach Awakening, Chögyam's appearance represented a serious setback. Nevertheless, even though the little boy's presence interrupted innumerable years of a long, calculated process of voluntary withdrawal which admitted no mistakes or delays, the old lama did not lose his focus and accepted the will Avalokiteshvara had communicated to him in a vision. In any case the lama was aware of the enormous effort he had to make, since as the solitary Buddha he had become, he was ready neither to preach nor to have disciples in his charge.

A ledge of rock was all he had as an altar. On it rested an offering bowl which he filled every morning and emptied in the evening, and a tiny statue of the Buddha carved in wood, modeled by the lama himself, as Chögyam would later find out. There was no trace of any Buddhist holy books, although they were not really necessary. The lama hermit knew the Pali Canon by heart—the Vinaya Pitaka, the Sutta Pitaka and Abhidhamma Pitaka—as well as a wide collection of the ancient texts full with philosophical commentaries.

"How old are you?"

"Five, master."

"Good. At your age I had already learned how to read and write both in Sanskrit and Tibetan, and had started the study of the *sutras*."

To begin with, he taught Chögyam how to prostrate himself before the image of the Buddha.

"Join your hands and place them first above your head, then at the level of your throat, and finally at your heart. This will help you purify your negative actions, whether physical or spiritual."

The old lama demonstrated, and Chögyam imitated every move, showing extreme solemnity in each of his gestures.

"Perfect," the old man said. "Now crouch and put the palms of your hands on the ground, then the knees and lastly your forehead. And always remember that besides being a physical exercise, prostrations must also involve a mental attitude."

Chögyam also learned to sit in the traditional lotus position, with legs crossed and each foot on top of the opposite thigh. In addition, the hermit showed Chögyam a simple mantra that he had to repeat many times a day.

"Prostrations and mantras will help you accumulate merit in your day to day life. Merit is the potential of positive energy we all have and which will lead you to obtain happiness and reach liberation."

Very often Chögyam did not understand some of the concepts the hermit explained, but he did not worry excessively since he knew the old man would repeat all the important ideas at the slightest opportunity. Over time Chögyam noticed that those teachings were sinking deep into him with the same efficiency and fixation as the vital advice ingrained in a child by his mother.

It took Chögyam very few weeks to learn by heart the invariable routine of the old lama. There were certain hours of the day in which he abandoned himself to a state of meditation so deep that he appeared to be dead—or at least dozing—and completely oblivious to anything happening in the outside world. But one day Chögyam discovered how mistaken he was, since what took place showed him that even in that state of trance the hermit never lost awareness of what was occurring around him.

Outside the snow was falling so heavily that it threatened to block the entrance to the cave. The old man opened his eyes suddenly, straightened himself, and gave Chögyam precise instructions: "Let's clear the entrance right away, or else we risk being buried by the snow."

The boy stood up at once and waited for his orders.

The lama handed him the alms bowl. "Use it to remove the snow."

Chögyam did as he was told and employed himself to throw the snow outside with the discipline of a worker bee. The old lama used only his bare hands to perform the task, as he had invoked tummo and the intense heat protected him from freezing. At times Chögyam would look at him out of the corner of his eye and stare in fascination at the lumps of snow melting between the old man's fingers, causing a light cloud of vapor to spiral up. They toiled for hours, since all the time they pushed the snow away from the entrance of the cave, the sky poured an infinity of thick snowflakes with equal intensity.

Winter gave them two more snowstorms of similar violence.

One morning when they were sitting opposite each other, in the middle of a lesson, Chögyam noticed a spider that had been crawling on the ground and soon began to climb up the lama's leg. The spider repulsed him. It was hairy and had at least four or five eyes. Yet the hermit seemed not to have noticed it. Chögyam kept on watching the spider as it began to run up the old man's torso and very soon reached his face. The lama went on talking, indifferent to the presence of the insect. The unusual situation distracted the boy from his master's words so much that in the end he decided to interrupt him. He pointed at the spider hesitantly. "You should kill it," he said.

"Chögyam, we Buddhists don't kill sentient creatures," the lama replied in a serene voice.

Chögyam raised his eyebrows in puzzlement. "And that includes spiders?"

"We consider the whole animal kingdom to be sentient beings, given that they can experience pleasure and pain."

"Master, I confess that I still don't understand how it matters so much to kill one single spider."

The old man pondered his answer. "Chögyam, do you remember the brief explanation I gave you of the concept of *samsara*?"

"Yes, master. Samsara is about the cycle of existence to which all individuals are bound."

"Animals too. Remember also that the constant rebirth of each one of us may lead us to a happy or painful existence depending on our karma."

"I don't follow, master."

"Very simple, Chögyam. You should know that besides the human condition, we are subject to numerous possible existences, like for example the animal."

Chögyam reflected on the words of the old man in silence. "Master, do you mean to say that this spider could be reborn as a man in a future existence?"

"Or he might have been one in a past life," the hermit pointed out.

Meanwhile, completely oblivious to this metaphysical debate, the spider continued its journey. It had gone back to the ground and now seemed to be heading straight for Chögyam's foot. He felt disgusted but did not move. A chill ran down his spine:

sentient or not, he would have stepped on it gladly. In the end the spider went past him and Chögyam breathed out in relief.

"Master, I would not like to be a spider in my next life," he confided with an unusually worried look.

The spontaneous commentary and his face, pale as wax, made the old man laugh heartily, perhaps for the first time in his forty years of retreat. When he had calmed down he said, "That won't happen if you fill your karma with good actions."

Not one day passed during that harsh winter without Chögyam remembering his parents with a knot in his throat and an emptiness in his heart. The pain caused by their loss was compensated by the hope of being reunited with Thupten some day. And he wished with all his might that wherever his older brother might be, he was safe and sound and in the care of good honest people.

A few days before winter took its leave until the next year, the hermit turned to Chögyam more solemnly than usual, sat before him and said, "Chögyam, I believe you are ready to accept the Buddha. It's about the act we call "taking refuge" according to the tradition of the way of dharma. Remember that this vow is not only taken for this life but it also takes into account your future lives, and if you should abandon the way, it would have negative consequences on your karma."

"Yes, master. I accept with great joy."

"Well, then repeat after me: I go to the Buddha's refuge; I go to the refuge of teaching; I go to the refuge of the community."

Chögyam did so, and his words resounded strongly against the walls of the cave. The old lama nodded in satisfaction, then cut off a small lock of the boy's hair as a sign of his total consecration to the Buddha.

"Very well. Now I must give you a name in dharma, a name that will be identified with your future Awakening. And given that you came to find shelter in my cave, which is my refuge, and as it's here that you've "taken refuge" you shall be known by the name of "the one who looks for refuge in the refuge.""

* * *

In the Tsurphu Monastery the senior monks were worried. Six years had gone by since the death of the Karmapa, and the tulku had not appeared yet.

Kyentse Rinpoche was in the library of the gompa looking for inspiration in the Dhammapada, a collection of concise verses of an ethical nature of which even a thorough reading did not help to shed any light on the matter. Kyentse, more and more frustrated, rolled the parchment up to return it to its place. As the late Karmapa's disciple he, more than anyone else, felt guilty at his inability to help find the reincarnation of his master.

Up to that date the committee of wise monks of which he himself was a member had done nothing but beat around blindly. The intuitions, visions, and dreams of the great gurus had so far led them to a dead end. There had been a number of false alarms. Some clues, mostly vague and imprecise, had led them to children who had been immediately discarded as the authentic tulku after the first preliminary tests.

Kyentse Rinpoche himself had made the pilgrimage on three occasions to Lake Yamdrok, which the Tibetans considered holy, in order to induce such visions and encourage his gifts of clairvoyance, but his long sessions of meditation on the shores of the Yamdrok turned out to be vain, and he had never received any inkling of the whereabouts of the tulku.

Nor were the astrologers and oracles consulted of any great help either, even though they boasted of high numbers of successful predictions and a time-honored tradition. The calculations, using very exact data as a basis, were repeated several times according to the position of the stars. But inexplicably every consultation gave a different prediction, without any agreement among them on the interpretation of the results.

They also had to be aware of omens, certain unusual phenomena that might take place at the birth of the tulku. In the region of Amdo, for example, a boy from a nomadic family was born under a shower of shooting stars. And the birth of another, in a remote hamlet near Tsochen, northeast of Lhasa, coincided with the blossoming of certain plants out of season. But once again, both candidates had been discarded as soon as they were visited.

It also might happen that the little tulku would show abilities or unusual behavior during his first years which would let him be identified. Perhaps the boy would know how a certain Buddhist ritual was performed without having ever been taught by anyone, or would simply sit for long periods of time without speaking. Yet in the present case nothing of notice had reached the ears of the committee, nothing special that deserved their attention.

Sometimes the events surrounding the death of the Karmapa might offer clues which would lead to the finding of his new incarnation. But Kyentse had gone over the events again and again without getting anywhere. There were also certain precedents according to which the Karmapa himself would leave a document before he died in which he described, more or less cryptically, the circumstances of his rebirth. But after going carefully through all the deceased's belongings, they had found no letter or document to this effect.

Kyentse took it all philosophically. He told himself that sooner or later there would be a sign, when they least expected it and from the most unsuspected place, which would guide them to the tulku once and for all. He was not going to be defeated by discouragement, for anxiety could be a serious enemy when he needed to keep his mind open and clear. Wise monks had to remain alert at all times so that any clues hidden in their dreams or visions would not pass unnoticed.

Tsultrim Trungpa walked into the library looking restless, as was usual in him. The abbot, as the one responsible for the Tsurphu Gompa, the official seat of the Karmapa, felt even more frustrated than Kyentse himself at the prolonged absence of legitimate authority at the Kagyu School. The false clues, the failed candidates and the obvious inability to locate the tulku after more than five years of trying had significantly undermined the abbot's spirit.

The political scene of the region, at least, seemed to have granted them pause. Prince Godan, the same one who had invaded Tibet causing an unprecedented blood bath, had later been impressed by the pacifist creed of the people of the land. In consequence he had summoned the most important Buddhist lama to his royal camp, located in the Chinese province of Gansu: the honor fell to Sa'gya

Pandita, leader of the Sakya School. The effect he produced on the Mongol executive officer, whom he captivated with his personality and powerful teachings and whom he even cured of a serious illness, was absolutely overwhelming.

On the other hand, the civil war between Kublai and Ariq Boke, Genghis Khan's two grandsons, for the title of Great Khan had been won by the former after three years of fratricidal fighting. This war also marked the end of the unified empire and the appearance of four independent khanates, each governed by a Khan and supervised by the Great Khan.

All these events, taken separately, should not have affected Tibet in any way, yet they did. The key to it all came when Prince Godan, one of the most loyal followers of Kublai Khan, told his lord about the qualities of Tibetan Buddhism which had so impressed him. To the surprise of many, his words didn't fall on deaf ears: the new emperor showed an interest in the fundamental points of that suggestive religion based beyond the Himalayas. The implications of that interest and its possible consequences for Tibet or the rest of the empire, however, were still impossible to foresee.

Tsultrim passed by Kyentse and greeted him with a nod. Neither of them felt their pride slighted, since both acknowledged the noble efforts of the Sakya School to safeguard the people of Tibet. Besides, they were sure that if the Karmapa had not passed away, the role of the Kagyu School in recent events would have been much more important.

Both schools had emerged in the 11th century as a consequence of the transfer of the Buddhist legacy from India, where Buddhism had been practically eradicated, mainly because of the Muslim invasions. The term "school" referred only to a particular lineage of masters and disciples, in which the teachings were transmitted from generation to generation. And, although it was true that each strand had its particular focus of dharma, in no case were there differences regarding the fundamental core.

The Sakya School was characterized by its eminently erudite nature. They contributed to the education of monks and nuns, the translation of classical Buddhist texts, and the composition of numerous treaties of exquisite brilliance. The founders, descendants of the first disciples of the Indian masters Padmasambhava and Shantarakshita, came from one of the ruling families.

The Kagyu School, on the other hand, emphasized the practice of meditation rather than the study of scripture and regarded oral transmission of the teachings between master and disciple as more important than anything else. This lineage could trace its origins back to the great translator Marpa and his mythical disciple Milarepa, one of the greatest contemplatives and religious poets of Tibet.

A sepulchral silence reigned in the library. The texts, written on long, thick pages and laid out on wooden covers, were wrapped in delicate cloths to prevent the pages from getting lost. The binding of books had never been a Tibetan custom. Kyentse Rinpoche and Tsultrim Trungpa exchanged looks devoid of artifice. Both of them had the feeling that sooner or later, the Kagyu School would come surprisingly to the fore in what was happening.

CHAPTER III

Spring

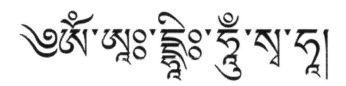

"He who lives by the charity of others is not merely a monk, but one who observes the code of behavior and thus becomes worthy of such a condition."

Dhammapada, 266

Spring arrived in fits and starts, as if it found it hard to take over from a reluctant, lazy winter, intent on prolonging its stay beyond Nature's ordinary limits.

The wintry season had followed its usual course at the Batang Monastery. The time the monks spent secluded behind its walls, protected from the vagaries of the weather, was devoted to deepening their meditation skills, carrying out the rituals of the temple, and intensifying the training of the novices, especially those who had taken up monastic life only recently.

Lobsang Geshe had put special effort into reeducating all those who, under the influence of Dechen's bad example, had relaxed the practice of Vinaya and strayed from the path of good behavior to which, as Buddhist monks, they had devoted their life. In particular, Lobsang had concerned himself with taking Lama Dechen in hand, and in fairness, the lama had shown his meekest face, always avoiding any confrontation with the abbot. But Lobsang did not trust Dechen's apparent docility. The precedents spoke for themselves. In fact, he was convinced that as soon as he began setting out on his usual trips throughout the region to preach the Buddha's teachings, the troublesome lama would once again take advantage of his absence to revert to his bad habits and challenge his authority.

For this reason Lobsang had decided to suspend his plan for the spring, which included a long journey through Kham with the aim of spreading the doctrine. Moreover, he would remain in Batang for an indefinite period, until he was absolutely certain he had quenched Dechen's rebelliousness for good.

Shortly before he shared his change of plans with the monks, something happened which confirmed that Lobsang had made the right decision.

One morning of the new spring, Lama Dechen strutted before Lobsang with his head held high and the hint of a malicious smile on his lips. At first sight Lobsang could make no sense of this behavior. Coming from Dechen, who never acted without an ulterior motive, it had to be one of his tricks. It was Dorjee who put him on the right track. The young monk told Lobsang to pay attention to the old lama's attire. Then he noticed. Dechen had added a new ornament in gold thread to his robe; although tiny, it really stood out on the cloth.

Now he could see the whole picture. By not complying with the rule which forbade any decoration on a monk's clothing, Dechen was openly defying him again, since he had no doubt that Lobsang would soon be leaving once again to carry out his missionary work.

Lobsang approached Dechen. Pointing at the brand new ornament on his robe he said, "I shall personally hold you to account for your flagrant breach of the rules at the next Uposatha ceremony."

Dechen's face underwent a radical transformation on hearing the unexpected news.

"You heard right," Lobsang went on as calmly as before. "This spring I shall stay at the monastery and renounce the long journeys I used to make at this time of year."

Since as far as food was concerned Buddhist monks relied completely on the lay faithful, with the arrival of spring they poured out into the streets every morning to beg. The Buddha considered begging to be the correct way of life for those men who devoted themselves to religious discipline, and the Batang Monastery, which was ruled by the principles of Theravada Buddhism, had kept up this sound habit.

The lay faithful took on their role honorably. They did not regard the Buddhist monks as beggars or tramps, but as devout men who had renounced material goods and devoted their lives to reach the highest level of inner progress. For that reason they contributed respectfully to their maintenance, incidentally rewarding themselves in the process with a worthy act which added to the balance of their karma.

There were two ways in which the monks could obtain food: by begging from door to door, or by accepting an invitation from a benefactor.

The monks left in stages throughout the morning, in small groups of three or four at the most. Lobsang had chosen three novices whom he himself would teach the rules and criteria they should follow in their begging. The apprentices were aged between twelve and twenty. Lobsang did not mind taking part in the training of the novices whenever his tight schedule would allow; he found it just as gratifying as his missionary activity. What he never normally did, however, was to take personal disciples. The duty of a master toward his pupil meant keeping a close relationship, comparable to that of a father and son, which involved teaching him the doctrine, giving him continuous advice and directing him appropriately along the way of dharma. Lobsang's wandering life had not allowed him to play the role of tutor with the dedication the situation required, and he more than anyone else knew that. The opposite extreme was personified in Lama Dechen, who took on as many pupils as he could, as if he wanted to mold them into his own image so as to count on as many supporters in the monastery as possible.

To begin with, Lobsang explained to the novices that there were some sectors of the city exclusively reserved to the bhikkhuni, from which they should keep a prudent distance. Once they had received this warning, they went out into the streets of Batang.

Each one had been given an alms bowl which they should always carry with them. This important item was used not only for receiving the food, but also for eating it. The bowls could be clay or iron, but never gold, silver, bronze, glass, or wood. The monks were supposed to handle them with extreme care, and only when they became damaged by use could they receive a new one from the community.

The novices accompanying Lobsang stood in front of a house and awaited his instructions.

"You must remain silent, standing outside the door for a reasonable length of time," Lobsang explained. "If you are given nothing, you should go elsewhere, avoiding at all times feelings of discontent, sadness or frustration."

Two minutes later a silhouette appeared at the window of the house. Before anyone came out, Lobsang added, "When food is placed in the bowl, you will accept it without considering its quality or quantity, or showing any kind of preference. You must also refrain from looking at the face of the donor, or even trying to identify whether it's a man or a woman."

Lobsang went away when an elderly lady opened the door of the house and watched from a distance how she placed a ball of tsampa in each of the novices' bowls. Next the woman turned and went back to her daily tasks, with a smile on her lips and her spirit soaring. Lobsang then returned to the novices.

"Remember, this is the only solid food you'll be able to eat all day," he warned them. "At first, fasting will seem hard, but you'll get used to it and it will no longer be a problem."

Lobsang went back to the monastery, where he gathered another group of novices to instruct in the same process. The new group repeated the same steps as the one before, but on this occasion the inhabitants of the house they stopped in front of invited them to come inside. For the lay faithful, an invitation meant a worthier action than a simple donation made at the door, besides being an unquestionable show of goodwill toward the community as a whole.

Lobsang accepted the invitation on behalf of the novices and clarified a few points as they went inside the house. They had to receive the food in their alms bowl and not on a regular plate. And as a sign of gratitude, they must recite before the donors some sutra which they had previously memorized. Lobsang, given his vast knowledge, would delight those present with some teaching of the Buddha's, something the novices were not yet ready to do. On that occasion he showed his gift for oratory, carefully expounding the twists and turns of the Four Noble Truths, which made up one of the basic pillars of Buddhist philosophy. Novices and benefactors ate in silence, all equally enjoying Lobsang's eloquence.

When the abbot was back at the monastery, convinced that he would not have to set foot in the city again that day, Dorjee told him that a layman had committed a fault worthy of the monks' reproach. The relationship between the monastic community and the society of faithful Buddhists was so close that both felt it legitimate to criticize each other for the improper behavior of any of their members. In this case it had been the monastic community which had singled out a faithful layman for his intolerable behavior. Apparently the person in question had made disrespectful comments about the Buddha and spoken slightingly of his teachings.

The punishment due, known as *patta nikujjana kamma*, was of a symbolic nature, although not without tangible consequences. A number of monks went to the transgressor's house, with Lobsang at their head, and once there they all turned their backs, alms bowls in their hands, as a sign that they would not accept anything from him and that the community did not acknowledge him as a faithful.

Minutes later, Lobsang made a sign and the monks left, after a crowd of curious onlookers had taken careful notice. Usually, from that moment on, the disgraced faithful could expect nothing but rejection by his neighbors and ultimately by a good part of the city. For the punishment to be withdrawn, it was enough for the monks if the man acknowledged his fault and sought forgiveness in public.

Lobsang walked back, mortified by guilt. From his point of view, the fact that a single follower should renounce the Buddhist creed meant that they, the monks, as guardians of the faith, were not doing enough. Each punishment given to a follower represented, deep down, a failure on their part, from which they should always draw a valuable lesson.

Lobsang had not forgotten Lama Dechen's last provocation, in the form of the golden ornament sewn onto his dress. So, when the first Uposatha ceremony of the spring took place, he made certain that it was carried out with the utmost rigor so that his effrontery would not go unpunished.

The monks took their places in the temple, sitting in rows facing each other, under the attentive look of the statues of the Buddhas and other divinities which filled the altars. The light inside the temple was dim; the wide hall, submerged in shadow, was dotted from one end to the other with the amber brightness of the yak-butter candles. Lobsang spoke to take attendance: participation by all the monks, except for the novices, was a fundamental prerequisite. There was only one absence which was found to be justified, and the monk in question, who was ill, had sent his "declaration of purity" with a fellow monk.

Satisfied with the count, Lobsang began a mantra, and all the other monks joined in at once. The sacred formula they repeated over and over again in their grave, deep voices managed to soothe their minds at the same time as it filled the hall with beneficial vibrations. After a while, Lobsang spoke again in order to recite the disciplinary code. According to procedure, after each set of rules had been listed, the monks who had committed some fault were supposed to confess before the community. It was a true examination of conscience, a check that guaranteed the effectiveness of the vows they had sworn on the day of their ordination. If the reading of a set of rules was followed by silence, it was assumed that nobody had infringed them.

When Lobsang recited the numerous rules which concerned clothing, nobody appeared to feel any personal reference. Lobsang then stood up and pointed at Lama Dechen, who was directly opposite him. "Dechen, isn't it true that you have violated the rule that forbids either dyeing or decorating our clothing? Had you forgotten, or were you expecting to pass over your fault?"

Part of the audience muffled a cry at the abbot's accusation.

Dechen stood up, but instead of acknowledging his fault, he confronted Lobsang openly. "I don't believe that a tiny thread of gold pinned to my chest infringes the spirit of the rule in any way."

Excitedly, the rest of the monks watched the dispute that had just begun. Dechen's reply opened the way to controversy. Dialectical debates were part of the essence of Buddhism itself and in fact formed one of the main tools used in the process of training the monks.

Lobsang picked up the glove and presented his arguments. "It's not the size of the ornament that matters, but its significance. The Buddha's teachings exhort us to banish vanity from our lives and to conduct ourselves according to the spirit of detachment. We must never lose sight of our goal, which is to move forward in the development of our inner progress."

Once again, Lobsang's lucidity and erudition had Lama Dechen and his weak reasoning on the ropes. Nevertheless, Dechen was an old dog in these matters and had already prepared an argument to counterattack with. "Vinaya not only permits our clothes to belong to us personally," he argued proudly, "but he also gives us the right to identify them, so that they don't get mixed up with the rest."

There was a discreet murmur of approval from the congregation. What Dechen had said was absolutely true. Although the lands, the monastery itself and everything in it belonged to the community, the monk's habit was considered to be the property of his owner, safe exceptional cases.

"What's your argument, then?" Lobsang reacted immediately. "That you have a right to wear the ornament because it's your own clothing, or that you wear it as a mark so that it's not mistaken for anybody else's?" Lobsang did not wait for a reply. The question was rhetorical. "The habit is yours, you're right. At least until it wears out and the community gives you a new one. But, on the one hand, if you want to mark it, it's obvious that you could do it on the lining, and nothing justifies it to be of gold. And on the other hand, Vinaya's maxim of prohibiting ornaments makes another absolutely essential point, which is precisely that through our clothing we make ourselves equal to everyone else in the community, including lamas, monks, and novices. Consequently the contradiction is not so much in Vinaya as in the twisted interpretation of its precepts that you insist on making."

Dechen's face had turned the color of Goji berries. In the eyes of all the other monks, it was clear that the abbot had come out resoundingly victorious in the fiery debate. Lobsang knew that he had perhaps been rather severe, but it was not simply because Dechen had brought it on himself. This was also the reason why he had made the decision to stay at the monastery: in order to make things absolutely clear to the old lama so that he would never kick over the traces again when Lobsang was away from Batang.

Even with all this, a humiliated and resentful Dechen insisted in adding one more ingredient to the already spent debate. "At least I don't infringe the rule about footwear!" he cried.

Vinaya forbade the monks to wear sandals inside the monastery, including the courtyard and the garden. The reason was no other than the noise made by the soles, which might disturb those in meditation. But it was no secret to anyone in the monastery that if Lobsang wore sandals it was because of a health problem, and that the soles of his feet were seriously worn away after his innumerable journeys throughout the remote villages of Kham spreading the teachings of the Buddha.

Lobsang did not even bother to reply. It was not worth it. The truth was that Dechen had done himself no favor, revealing the darkness inside him and exposing his poisoned soul to the sight of all.

At Tenzin's request, the abbot agreed to go to the neighboring city of Litang to put his wide knowledge at the nun's service. The trip was short, and he would not be away from the monastery more than a week. Besides, the occasion deserved it: the leader of the bhikkhuni was intent on opening a new convent in Litang, a town where there were no Buddhist nuns.

Dorjee and three other young monks went with Lobsang, while Tenzin's retinue consisted of two other nuns from her order. Dorjee aspired to become a lama in the near future. He spared no effort in his studies, which were filled with metaphorical and spiritual content, nor in hours dedicated to the most intense meditation. Whenever he could, he stuck to Lobsang like a limpet, in order to soak himself in his wisdom and advice. Dorjee took advantage of the trip to exchange impressions with Lobsang about the *Chöd* ritual, a deep meditative exercise carried out at night and alone, and whose surroundings were the heart of a graveyard. Lobsang resolved the doubts of the young monk who, emboldened by his suggestions, decided to put the exercise into practice that same spring.

During the journey, Tenzin thanked Lobsang profusely for his commitment to suppressing Lama Dechen's attempts to damage the reputation of the bhikkhuni. In fact, Lobsang's warnings had been enough to stop the ugly rumors Dechen had spread. Similarly, there had been no more problems with the sharing out of the areas for the alms rounds.

"If I decided to stay in Batang this spring," Lobsang said, "it was to resolve this feud with Dechen once and for all. And one way or another, I won't rest until I've succeeded."

A group of benefactors of Litang had promised to finance the building of the convent, having given up several properties for the purpose. But just as the moon needs a cloudless night to show off her brightness, the Buddhist temple requires an appropriate setting to display all its influence. For that reason integrating the architecture into the landscape was not enough; the deep forces of the earth itself also had to be considered, not to mention the spirits who populated valleys, mountains and rivers, so as to avoid disturbing their harmony as far as possible.

Lobsang studied the land carefully. The setting, in relation to the built-up area, was suitable: on the outskirts, far enough to avoid the bustle of the city, but not so much as to dissuade the lay faithful from visiting and taking part in the religious life through prayer and offerings.

Lobsang walked around, stretching his neck and looking first in one direction and then the other, weighing up the possibilities of the setting. Tenzin followed restlessly, almost stepping on his feet.

"Tradition lists a series of general characteristics the setting should have," he pointed out. "A high mountain behind, many hills in front, two rivers flowing from right and left, and a valley opening up the view."

Tenzin paled at hearing this list of requirements.

"Don't worry." Lobsang laughed. "Everybody knows they can't always be fulfilled."

"And what else should we take into account?" Tenzin asked, slightly relieved.

"We must pay attention to the signs. For example, is there a spring nearby?"

"Yes. There's one to the left."

"Perfect." Lobsang clapped. "A spring on either side symbolizes an offering cup. It's a good omen. On the other hand, if it had been under the monastery it would mean a crack in the bottom of a container."

"What else?" Tenzin urged.

"The routes of access. A road from the southeast of the monastery signifies friends and support, whereas a road to the northeast foretells the arrival of enemies and demons."

"Here the road comes from the east," Tenzin said.

"It will do," Lobsang replied with a smile.

Next the abbot bent over and carefully studied the soil under his feet.

"What are you looking for?

"Anthills," Lobsang replied. "It would be a terrible sign if there were any."

At once the group of monks and nuns who accompanied the expedition knelt down and scrutinized every inch of soil with the same care a physician might use to examine a patient. They did not have to wait long for the good news. In general terms, what stood out was an apparent lack of insects.

"I don't see any thorny bushes around, either," Lobsang said. "That's good, isn't it?"

"A must." Lobsang arched his eyebrows and reflected for a few minutes more. "Let's carry out one more test. The definitive one."

Lobsang told Dorjee and the others to dig a hole, knee-deep. "And make sure the sides are smooth."

"What does the test consist of?" Tenzin wanted to know.

"When they're finished, we'll fill the hole with water and move a hundred paces away. When we come back if the water has kept its level without seeping through, it'll mean the omen is favorable."

The test had aroused great expectations among the monks and nuns. Tenzin held her breath while the test was carried out according to Lobsang's instructions. First they walked away and then retraced their steps, to find on their return that the water had stayed there, so that Tenzin felt an incredible surge of joy.

"Congratulations," Lobsang said. "This place has the right conditions for you to build your Buddhist convent."

"Thank you so much," Tenzin murmured, still moved.

"One more thing," Lobsang added. "Before you begin to build, don't forget to perform a ceremony of protection. For that, bury several sealed vessels in the ground, filled with grain and holy offerings."

When Lobsang went back to the monastery, Dechen was more furious than ever. The old lama could not bear the fact that the bhikkhuni were spreading throughout the region, still less that Lobsang was actively helping the nuns in their plans for expansion.

* * *

Thupten survived the winter, in spite of the many calamities he suffered in his own flesh.

With the passing of time he had assumed that the next years of his life, his future in the short and medium term, would be spent with Wangchuk, the ruthless outlaw who had dragged him along with him conceding him the privilege of being a witness to his miserable existence. In his most private thoughts Thupten yearned to grow up overnight and confront Wangchuk as a strong young man, so that he could free himself from his tyranny in a man-to-man fight. But in the meantime he was still a child who had only just turned seven, who had even banished from his mind the idea of escaping from the outlaw: partly because of the terror he inspired in him and partly because he did not know where to go or what to do with his life.

Out of need, and because he had no other choice, Thupten had gotten used to frequenting the squares of Batang and other places full of passers-by, made to beg as though he were a cripple to provide for Wangchuk and his insatiable love of drink. Living with the outlaw had made Thupten develop a sixth sense, or in other words, hone his intuition to the point where he could distinguish those moments when he would be wise to hold his tongue from those others when Wangchuk welcomed his chatter. In this way he evaded more than one beating, thanks to his perception, even though there were some he could not avoid no matter what he might or might not have done, since nothing escaped Wangchuk's rage and the bitter frustration which devoured him from within.

Thupten recalled his past in the hamlet as if it were far distant in time, more like a dream than reality, even though he was aware that his mind was playing tricks on him. Not a day went by without thoughts of his family coming to his mind, even though it frightened him to notice that their faces were fading little by little among the mists of memory.

Wangchuk represented the other side of the coin: he was more than pleased with himself for finding the boy, thanks to whose begging he could pay for the beer with which he drowned the sorrows of the abandoned life he had condemned himself to live. However incredible it might sound, Wangchuk had even convinced himself that Thupten had been very lucky to have been found. After all, he had taken the boy under his wing and given a meaning to his life.

The arrival of spring forced them to leave the cabin that had been their shelter during the winter. The shepherds had reclaimed it as soon as they brought their herds out to graze in the plains.

So it was that Wangchuk and Thupten moved to a grove of evergreen oaks behind the graveyard, where they took advantage of the offerings of food left by visitors at their ancestors' graves. The hardness of the Tibetan soil did not allow the burial of the deceased, with the exception of criminals, minors, pregnant women, and those who had died of contagious illnesses, all of whom suddenly became Thupten's new neighbors. The rest of the population could expect the traditional and brutal sky burial, preceded by the dismemberment of the corpse and rounded off by the bloody feast the vultures made of the remains. They spent the nights, which were milder already, under the stars and the treetops, warmed by the flames of a fire and wrapped in thick yak furs.

It was around that time when Thupten noticed some strange men in the city for the first time. They wore saffron-colored tunics and went from house to house with lowered heads, begging for food in a small bowl. Wangchuk, looking at them with half-closed eyes and furrowed brow, told Thupten that they were Buddhist monks, representatives of Tibet's new religion, which had replaced the old Bön tradition. When the boy wanted to know more about the beliefs or customs of those silent monks, the outlaw answered him roughly, referring to them as stupid shaven-headed religious rabble, and threatened him with a good beating if he ever mentioned them in his presence again.

Thupten got the message the first time, for quite apart from his warning, the deep hatred in Wangchuk's gaze spoke for itself.

There was a reason for the outlaw's aversion. From his twisted point of view, the Buddhist monks were the cause of his disgrace. But that interpretation, apart from being one-sided, was anything but realistic. The truth was that no matter what Wangchuk might think, the theft which had caused him to lose one hand had been perpetrated in no less a place than the Batang Temple. Emboldened by alcohol and its illusory effects, he had stolen holy ornaments of gold and silver whose value in coin was even greater than the merely spiritual. Hence the abbot's accusation had been made as soon as the robbery was discovered.

The rest of the story was not hard to imagine: it was not long before the authorities arrested Wangchuk when they surprised him trying to sell the stolen objects to a merchant caravan on its way through the city.

Paradoxically, several months later Wangchuk had tried to join the order without revealing his identity, hoping to find a solution to all his problems. But to his disgrace he was rejected, which increased his aversion to the damned Buddhist monks whom he blamed for the amputation of his hand. Wangchuk was probably unaware that it had not even been anything personal, simply a decision based on the principles laid out in the Vinaya, according to which certain candidates had to be excluded, particularly debtors, deserters, and outlaws. Under no circumstances could the monastic community become a refuge for malefactors wishing to hide from society and avoid punishment.

So Thupten refrained from asking questions about the Buddhist monks and contented himself with watching them from afar, always intrigued by their looks and peculiar behavior.

By then Wangchuk already felt sure enough of Thupten to leave him alone, without having to keep a constant eye on him. He knew the boy had already assumed his destiny and would not try to escape even if he saw the opportunity.

"You stay here," he warned him.

Thupten had noticed that once a week, always at the same time, shortly after noon, Wangchuk would leave without saying where he was going and with an enigmatic smile on his lips. The outlaw would disappear in the woods, while Thupten waited for him to come back under the grove of evergreen oaks they had made into their shelter, and which could hardly have been called a home.

Thupten's eyes followed the outlaw until his figure was lost in the grove. Then he stood up, stretched his neck so as not to lose him and took a couple of steps in the same direction. Thupten had decided to go after him, spurred by curiosity, to discover the secret of those mysterious daytime outings from which Wangchuk always came back not only showing his more relaxed side, but even with a certain air of restrained satisfaction.

Thupten followed him stealthily. At first it turned out to be quite a complicated business, as the foliage was sparse and barely offered any cover from the furtive glances of the outlaw, who now and then would look in every direction to make sure he was completely alone. But as Wangchuk went further away from the graveyard and into the depths of the wood, the bushes and undergrowth became Thupten's allies in his zeal to stay undiscovered.

Thupten felt quite nervous, although not enough to abandon his risky adventure. He knew that if Wangchuk caught him the beating would be a memorable one, so he took the greatest care with every step, trying to avoid either the creaking of a twig or the rustle of fallen leaves on the ground. On one occasion Thupten nearly lost Wangchuk's trail when the outlaw, turning suddenly, disappeared from his sight. Luckily, a few seconds later the rags that made up his outline appeared through the woodland, allowing Thupten to continue his pursuit from the point where he had left it.

Minutes later Thupten noticed that Wangchuk was slowing down. The outlaw went on a few more yards, moving very carefully, and hid behind a particularly thick tree trunk. From there he glanced several times at whatever was in front of him. Thupten stopped too, but as he could only see Wangchuk's back, he strained to try and pick sounds out of the silence. He was soon able to hear two different sets of murmurs: one, that of a river; the other, a chorus of female voices.

Thupten moved parallel to the outlaw's left and covered the few paces that separated him from the edge of the wood. There he dropped to the ground and hid in the undergrowth. His view of the scene could not have been better. The course of a river of calm turquoise water, deep amid nature, flowed through the woods, forming a peaceful haven. A group of women milling around the shore broke the bucolic harmony of the surroundings, even though all they were doing was whispering among themselves.

What caught Thupten's attention was that these women wore the same saffron-colored dress as the Buddhist monks he had seen in the city, the ones he barely knew anything about, since Wangchuk either refused to talk about them or simply cursed them through his teeth, grimacing scornfully as he did so. The bhikkhuni, whose convent was nearby, came to the river to bathe once a week in the belief that the spot was remote enough to give them absolute privacy.

The nuns began to undress little by little, and soon their inaccessible bodies were revealed. Although pale and unembellished, they were still beautiful and suggestive thanks to the healthy vigor of most of them. Thupten watched them, filled with curiosity but without a drop of lust. He was still too much of a child to understand the mysteries of carnal desire or feel the heat of the lower instincts, those mechanisms which can bend the will of the most tenacious man so as to satisfy his darkest desires.

Thupten looked to his right, where Wangchuk, totally unaware of the boy's presence, was spying on the women with his tongue hanging out and eyes like saucers. But that was not all he was doing. Thupten noticed that the outlaw had taken his member out and appeared to be stroking it with his only hand. And it did not seem to the boy that he had the intention to urinate, as would have been logical.

The meaning of the scene around Thupten, however obvious it might be, completely escaped his unsullied, childish mind. Nevertheless, he still had his intuition—a sense which had saved his skin more than once during his time with the outlaw—and it told him that there was danger in the situation, and that if he wished to stay safe he had better flee as soon as possible and forget the strange events he was witnessing.

Thupten was getting ready to crawl out of there, but before he could move a single muscle a sound to his left made him stop short. He remained silent, listening for any sound no matter how small, until his ear caught a wheezing breath. It seemed that Wangchuk was not the only spectator of this unusual show. With the utmost caution, Thupten peered through the thicket toward where he guessed the source of the wheezing was hidden. It did not take him long to find it. It was an old man, quite wrinkled, huddled behind a tree as if his life depended on it. Thupten's surprise was double: firstly because the tunic worn by the voyeur identified him as a Buddhist monk, and secondly because like Wangchuk, this other man also had his member out for no apparent reason.

If one thing was clear in Thupten's mind, it was that the sooner he vanished the better. Something told him that he would pay for his audacity dearly if either of the men, the outlaw or the

Buddhist monk, found him poking his nose into their business. He set off in the opposite direction to the way he had come, concentrating above all on not making any telltale noise. He crept like a caterpillar, dragging his clothes—they had been rags for quite a while—along the ground, which was full of insects and covered with mud in quite a few places. As he did so his heart beat so hard he was afraid the noise would give him away.

He only allowed himself a single glance over his shoulder, to check that the two onlookers were where he had left them: about sixty feet away from each other, but neither of them aware of the other's presence. He continued crawling through the bushes, then when he had covered a safe distance, he stood up and ran as if possessed until he reached the oak wood by the graveyard.

When Wangchuk came back, Thupten was trembling from head to toe, thinking that the outlaw would only need to look at his face to know what he had done. Thupten closed his eyes and waited in terror for the first blow, but in the end it never came. In fact, when he opened his eyes again he saw Wangchuk lying on the grass, ready to take a nap, with an expression of complete satisfaction on his face.

Wangchuk used to repeat, rather archly, that living next to the graveyard had its advantages too, particularly the tranquility of the place, whose idyllic peace allowed them to sleep soundly all night through. Thupten nodded and preferred not to mention the stench of decomposing bodies which the draughts spread around or the absence of a roof over their heads. Silence, on most occasions, had become Thupten's greatest ally.

One night, though, a strange moaning woke them up in the middle of the night, pulling them out of a deep sleep. Wangchuk and Thupten looked at each other wonderingly. It was an unusually dark night, with the moon on the wane and the stars devoid of their usual brilliance. A grave voice, coming from the graveyard, echoed through the wood amid the surrounding silence, with a thunderous echo. To the ears of the outlaw this unfathomable chant was not only incomprehensible but it sent sinister shivers up his spine. Wangchuk summoned up what courage he could and got up, ready to search out the origin of the mystery.

"Come with me," he whispered to Thupten.

Wangchuk would never have admitted it, but at that moment he was genuinely terrified that some loathsome demon might have caused a dead man to rise from his tomb and was having fun at his expense.

The outlaw forced himself to walk toward the graveyard, followed by Thupten, who felt more curious than anything else. Soon a human form appeared, half-hidden in the shadows and barely outlined in the darkness. Wangchuk was relieved to find it was a man of flesh and bone, or at least that's what he deduced from his everyday appearance and his unthreatening attitude. The eccentric individual was sitting on the ground, making intricate movements with his hands and intoning some kind of apparently endless prayer. Two unmistakable features, recognizable even in the blackness of the night, enabled Wangchuk to identify him as a Buddhist monk: his clean-shaven head and the style of his cloak banished any doubt in that respect.

Dorjee, deep in meditation, had fallen into a deliberate trance while he performed the complex Chöd ritual. The young monk kept his eyes closed, recited mantras in Sanskrit, and was completely oblivious to everything around him. There was a reason for this gloomy setting, which also played a part in the performance.

The Chöd ritual was a tantric practice that involved a great deal of preparation. Whoever performed it had to visualize the methodical dismembering of his own body, from the eyes to the limbs, including the guts and internal organs. Then, following that process of visual imagery even deeper, the separate parts of the organism, fragmented and atomized to the utmost degree, were poured into a pot of boiling water, and the final contents were offered to all sentient beings to satisfy their yearnings and as a display of compassion. To the loneliness and the funereal nocturnal atmosphere must be added the diabolic deities which, according to popular belief, gathered at the site to disrupt the ceremony. The hideous, repulsive ritual symbolized the contemplative's renunciation of the thing he held most dear: his own body. Ultimately, that exercise meant the banishment of the ego from the mind of the Buddhist and an important step in his detachment from everything connected with the material world. Nevertheless, the test was no mere formality, and it was well known that not everybody was able to complete it successfully. Some aspiring ritualists, overpowered by the ritual itself and the illusion created in the abyss of their minds, became overcome by panic and ended, if not deranged, directly killed by terror.

Having solved the mystery, Wangchuk clicked his tongue and shook his head, resigned to spending the rest of the night suffering the torture of those prayers. He could challenge the monk and try to scare him away, but he knew it would be unwise unless he wanted to get into trouble. The influence of the Buddhist monastic community in the society of Batang was not something to be taken lightly.

So Wangchuk turned and went back into the oak wood. Thupten on the other hand did not move from the spot. The boy was fascinated by the rhythm of the mantras, the twisting of the hands, and in general the electric energy given out by the amazing ritual. Finally Thupten gave himself up to sleep, lost in rapt contemplation of the mysterious monk and the spectral halo of mist which shrouded his silhouette. But as soon as dawn brought him back to reality after touching his face with the first light of day, he saw that the graveyard was empty; no trace remained of the intrepid Buddhist.

Weeks went by and Wangchuk began to notice that the hand-outs Thupten received were progressively shrinking. At first he thought the boy was not making the same effort as before, or even that he might be skimming off part of the benefits. However, he soon discarded both reasons after checking on him exhaustively for several days in a row. He realized the boy had nothing to do with the alarming reduction in the donations received from the inhabitants of Batang. The outlaw went on to draw a direct connection between the losses suffered and the presence of the Buddhist monks throughout the city.

"Damn them!" he muttered.

Soon it was very clear to him. The problem had not been noticeable in winter, since the monks stayed within the walls of their monastery. But come spring, as soon as they poured into the streets again, the consequences began to be felt. Now people carried less money on them, because some of the coins which filled their pockets were being spent on food which later made its way to the monks begging from door to door. Wangchuk was furious: the disloyal competition from the monks was threatening to ruin his way of life.

The outlaw began to worry more and more, until one morning, when he met a group of them on their usual rounds, a brilliant idea suddenly came into his mind. Sometimes the monks were accompanied by children, very young novices, who followed exactly the same procedure as the adults. *If you can't beat them, join them,* he thought. His idea might be very simple, he had no doubt, but it might also be extremely effective.

Wangchuk was well aware that any initiative contrary to the law carried a sanction, and this case was no different. To pretend to be a Buddhist monk constituted a crime of misappropriation, equivalent to fraud or theft, and was punished with the same severity. But Wangchuk was not thinking of risking his own neck at all; being left with one hand had been enough. The risk would be borne by Thupten alone.

"Today we're going to follow the monks we see in the street and analyze their conduct," Wangchuk said.

"Why?" Thupten asked in surprise. "Up till now you wanted nothing to do with them."

"Don't answer back and do as I say."

They spent the rest of the morning watching different groups of monks following their daily routine. Wangchuk was glad to see that just as he had suspected, they did not seem to do anything out of the ordinary. Apparently they just stopped at a house, holding a bowl they never let go of, and simply waited dumbly for someone to offer them some food. It was rare for them to come away empty-handed.

Wangchuk planned his strategy while they were going back to the oak wood. As soon as day broke, before the streets came to life and filled with passers-by, Thupten would beg for food at the houses posing as a little Buddhist monk. With whatever he got they would have enough for food, and as for the coins the boy got afterward by begging in the squares, however few of them there might be, Wangchuk could always waste them on beer.

The outlaw told Thupten his plan with a wide insincere smile, presenting it as the solution to all their problems.

But Thupten, somewhat less naive than when he had first met him, expressed his doubts about the dangers of the plan Wangchuk had put forward. "And if they find me out pretending to be a Buddhist monk?"

"Nothing will happen to you," the outlaw lied. "At most you'll just be reprimanded."

Wangchuk now had to deal with the logistics and mechanics of the operation. The first requirement—and probably the most complicated one—was to get hold of a monk's habit. For this he used nothing less than some scraps of material he found lying in a corner of the graveyard, remains of shrouds which when badly sewn together became a tunic made to Thupten's measure. To dye the cloth he used natural dyes from flowers and tree bark, until after several failed attempts he finally managed to get an orange shade which to profane eyes could pass for the original color.

"It fits like a glove," the outlaw said as Thupten put on the stinking garment made of waste.

The second indispensable thing was the alms bowl. Wangchuk solved this problem much more expeditiously: he stole a wooden bowl from a stall in the market while the craftsman was not looking. The bowl was meant to be a censer, but it was Wangchuk who would decide its function, not the hands which had shaped it.

Last but not least was the shaving of Thupten's head. For that Wangchuk used the old knife he had for cutting meat, a blunt piece of rusty metal he wielded clumsily. With this he tugged sharply at the hair with no trace of compassion, while Thupten bit his tongue so as not to scream from the pain and two big tears fell down his cheeks like drops of blood. When Wangchuk had finished his work Thupten's skull emerged covered in cuts, and his ears jutted out on each side of his head more noticeably than ever.

With all the preparations complete, they went to the city next day at first light.

"You know what you have to do, right?"

Thupten nodded.

"Good," Wangchuk said. "And don't forget, if there's any trouble, don't you ever mention my name. You don't know me. I'm warning you, or else I'll make you pay dearly afterward."

Without more ado, the outlaw chose a house at random, left Thupten standing in front of the door, and went to hide round the corner, looking forward to the success of his master plan. A woman came out a few minutes later and stood there in astonishment looking Thupten up and down, wondering if this were some kind of joke in bad taste. The bowl he carried was made of wood, the pretended robe was an insult to her intelligence and to cap it all, she knew for sure that the Buddhist monks would never leave a novice as young as that on his own.

Fuming, the woman turned and disappeared behind her door without a word. All things considered, Thupten could be thankful that she had not tried to report him.

Wangchuk grabbed Thupten by the arm and dragged him into an alley. "What on earth did you do to make everything go so wrong?!"

"I just did what you told me."

The outlaw, filled with rage and unable to accept the failure of his great idea, shook Thupten like a broken doll and then gave him a push that threw him against the wall.

Thupten crouched on the ground, ready for the rain of blows that was on its way. He had learned that sometimes, even though it was not his fault, Wangchuk took it out on him.

That, now, was the life which had fallen to him as his lot.

* * *

The first flowers that came up through the cracks of the rocks announced the arrival of spring.

Chögyam came out of the cave one morning and contemplated in fascination the transformation the monotonous winter landscape had undergone. The mountains shone on the horizon now, reflecting a livelier and more energetic sun which at moments hid behind a retinue of wispy clouds. At his feet stretched the steep hillside, flooded by the melted snow which ran in rivulets through the grass and ended in the cedar woods at the foot of the mountain. Above the cave the frozen brook flowed again, filling the place with a hypnotic murmur that encouraged relaxation. Further up, among the rocks as far as the limits of his vision, there spread a blanket of low scrub and all kinds of bushes. The animals, absent during the winter season, had also decided to leave their shelters.

The birds warbled, the butterflies flew around the bushes, and the rodents peered out and hid again with astonishing speed.

The cold temperatures also mellowed. But during the first week, as happened every year and as the hermit knew so well, life inside the cave became unbearable because of the thaw. Snow melted and filtered through cracks and clefts in the cave, endless streams of water slid down the ceiling and walls, forming rivers which made puddles on the floor and filled the entrance with mud.

"We'll sleep outside for a few days," the hermit said.

"Yes, master."

Chögyam took it as an adventure, only feeling a little afraid when he heard wolves marauding through the mountains howling at the moon and fighting among themselves.

The hermit valued Chögyam's progress in the learning of dharma very highly. The problem was something different. The old man was worried about the way the boy's health had worsened as a result of the relentless diet they shared. Chögyam had not even complained, but the physical decline he had shown since his arrival at the cave was unmistakable. Luckily the hermit knew the mountain well and how to enrich the boy's diet now that spring had arrived. He would have to wait a little longer, but soon he would be able to give him wild fruits like those of the apricot tree, as well as vegetables, mainly turnip and white radish which grew wild in other areas of the mountain. The leaves of the turnip alone were extremely rich in nutrients: protein, fiber, and large quantities of calcium.

Greater hygiene also played its part in improving the externals of Chögyam's life. Now he could wash his dirty rags in the clear water brook and also rinse his own body, which had been covered till now with a thick layer of dirt and grime.

On one of those days of the new season Chögyam turned six years old, but as his parents were not there to tell him he was not even aware of the fact. The hermit, for his part, had lost count of his years a long time ago in his commitment to raising his level of consciousness and reaching the state of complete liberation.

The bond between the hermit and Chögyam had strengthened with time, but the hermit lama had raised an emotional barrier which prevented the development of a deeper affection, beyond the strict relationship between a master and his disciple.

Focused on his work of teaching, the hermit took advantage of the arrival of good weather to continue Chögyam's preparation in a different setting. So one morning he led him out of the cave to teach him how to meditate. They walked around the mountain until they reached the north face and stopped at a ledge which extended several yards over the abyss. If simply looking at that thin sheet of rock was frightening, walking along it was even more so.

The hermit stepped along the narrow roof of the precipice and stood at the very edge.

"This is the perfect spot to initiate you into the techniques of meditation," he said flatly.

Evidently Chögyam did not share the same opinion. He had turned pale, and a cold sweat covered his hands and forehead. A terrible vertigo, the direct result of the tragedy his family had suffered on the mountain pass, had paralyzed his mind.

The hermit sat on the ground and gestured to Chögyam to sit beside him. The lama's serene movements and the confidence of his words managed to unblock Chögyam's immobility. A few timid steps led him to the bold seat the master had chosen.

From that point they looked over the high plateau, sprinkled with an infinite number of granite boulders, layered slate, and blue quartz. Far below them at the bottom of the abyss ran a river of dark water, forming whirlpools of spray at the foot of the waterfalls. And above their heads as a roof, there was an immaculate sky with thin clouds they could have touched if they had reached far enough up with their arms.

Chögyam closed his eyes and sat in the lotus position with the back of his hands on his legs.

"Pay attention, Chögyam, meditation is the fundamental axis of Buddhism, our most important practice. You will learn to observe your mind and keep it relaxed and alert at the same time."

Chögyam nodded, even though the feeling of being suspended in the air thousands of miles high had filled his stomach with butterflies.

"Begin by reciting a mantra," the hermit told him. "Your favorite one of all those I've taught you."

Chögyam did as he was told and gradually began to relax.

"That's it. Now you must concentrate and fix your attention on a single point. And that point will be the sound of your own mantra."

The hermit remained silent for a few minutes, letting Chögyam become one with the sound of his voice.

"Next, pay attention to your body, to your sensations. Let nothing escape your control."

Chögyam felt the touch of the breeze on his face, breathed in the mountain air, and tuned in to the rhythm of his own breathing.

"Secondly, attend to your emotions," the hermit said. "What is your present state of mind? Do you feel happy or sad? Serene or nervous? Compassionate or angry?"

Chögyam searched the nooks and crannies of his mind, isolating emotion after emotion until he had identified them all.

"Finally, direct your concentration to your thoughts and quiet your mind. Thoughts come and go in an instant. The mind is restless, volatile, like a wild horse you have to tame."

Once again the hermit let a while go by before coming to the last part of the exercise.

"Now use the creative skill of your mind and imagine you are making generous offerings to the Buddha on bright silver platters. Visualize it and create your own symbolic universe. Allow yourself to be enveloped by the iconography you have built in your mind and reproduce the image in an infinite cycle of times."

A few minutes later the hermit rose without a sound, stealthily as a cat, to make his way back.

But Chögyam was not long in noticing and, interrupting his process of meditation, he cried out: "Master, don't leave me here alone!"

The hermit lama stopped and smiled broadly. "Excellent, Chögyam," he said with satisfaction. "I was testing you, and you've done exceptionally well. You've shown that despite your great concentration, your mind was still alert. From now on we'll come here daily to meditate on this ledge, and we'll do it in the cave too. Constant practice will leave its mark inside you and with time, you'll raise your level of consciousness."

"What does that mean, master?"

The hermit thought for a moment. "Well, for example, you'll be able to see the black hat I wear on my head."

Chögyam looked at him in surprise. Most certainly there was no hat there. But the master did not usually joke, least of all about things like this.

"I've been wearing it since I picked you up from the bottom of the valley," he added. "Don't forget that samsara, the reality we're trapped within in the cycle of existences, is nothing more than pure illusion, and we only begin the Awakening when we're capable of opening our consciousness and seeing the true nature of things."

Chögyam was still not wholly convinced. "A black hat, master? Are you sure about what you're saying?"

"Of course. And when you're capable of seeing it, then you'll be the wearer in turn."

The hermit also took his moments of rest and relaxation, which were necessary after his marathon sessions of meditation and elaborate exercises, both tantric and esoteric. His love of wood-carving was always an unsurpassed means of escape during his long time of seclusion. With the help of a gouge, a kind of chisel mounted on a wooden handle, which was the only tool he had allowed himself to bring from the monastery, he spent hours carving until out of a rough wooden block he brought forth a beautiful figure, which afterward came to decorate his humble altar in the cave.

His latest creation had been a six-armed Mahakala, an irate divinity and protector of dharma which had delighted Chögyam with the ferocious detail of the teeth and the remarkable weapons it wielded in his hands. Over the last few days, though, Chögyam had noticed that whenever the hermit lama took up his carving, he always turned his back to him so as to hide his work from view. In the end, and despite his gnawing curiosity, Chögyam decided to respect his master's desire.

The hermit also practiced yoga both inside and outside the cave. The exercise was tremendously useful as a counterbalance to the many hours he spent sitting, but also contributed to alleviate any back problems and, it goes without saying, had allowed him to reach his present age in such an enviable physical state.

Chögyam tried to imitate his master's postures, but there was one in particular that defeated him no matter how hard he tried. The "posture on the head," as it was called, involved standing on one's head with one's forearms resting on the floor. In this manner, which is to say upside down, many benefits were apparently obtained, such as improvement of blood circulation, perfect redistribution of the energetic fluid, and the relief of migraines and chronic fatigue. Yet even though he exerted himself like a mule, Chögyam could not maintain this particular posture. In fact, he fell down so often that the hermit could not stop laughing at this repertoire of falls and thuds on the part of his stubborn disciple.

After several weeks of meditation on the rock ledge on the north side of the mountain, Chögyam excitedly confided to the hermit that he had experienced his first vision. "Master, I saw the outline of a person coming toward me, walking through dense fog. And although the face was blurred in the mist, I have no doubt it was a woman."

"Go on."

"I think it was my mother, because she gave me a radiant smile and offered me a piece of tu, the delicious cheesecake she used to make. What can it mean, master?"

"You know what, Chögyam? I don't think it was your mother who really visited you after all, but a *dakini*. Dakini are female Buddhist spirits who live in the skies and on the mountaintops, and who manifest themselves in visions, dreams, and contemplative experiences. They have great power, and always aid those who give up their lives to retreat and meditation. I've always felt the protective warm cloak of the dakini very close to me, and without their saving presence I would never have survived here alone all these years. They gave me the black hat I've told you about, although they warned me it wasn't for me."

"Why did they appear to me?"

"I'd say they want you to know you have their blessing."

On the way back, while disciple and master continued their exchange of opinions, something caught their attention beside a curtain of shrubs. It was the freshly killed remains of some animal, the prey of a snow leopard. The hermit bent over the remains and began to scoop them up.

"What are you doing, master?"

"I'm taking them, and later we'll eat them. You're growing and it will be good for you to eat some meat."

"But can we do that after what you explained to me about living creatures?"

"You don't need to worry, Chögyam," the hermit said with absolute conviction. "As long as we don't kill the animal, we're not breaking any mandate by eating its remains."

The revelations and experiences followed one after another, and Chögyam was constantly surprised. The most extraordinary of them occurred one afternoon when Chögyam had gone to gather wild fruits and on returning came across a vision which left him speechless, his knees trembling like icicles.

When he entered the cave he saw the hermit in his usual lotus position, but this time he was suspended in midair a foot above the floor. Chögyam, his eyes nearly popping out of his head, muffled a cry, and with the shock the fruit he was carrying fell all over the cave floor. The hermit seemed to be in a kind of mystical ecstasy and did not even notice the boy's presence.

In the end Chögyam left the cave and did not come back until the hermit had recovered his normal state. Afterward, when he had told him what he had seen, the hermit lama made little of the event, and explained that only through ecstasy as an exceptional state of consciousness could one understand vacuity, so that when he looked into the void, into *sunyata*, the waves of ecstasy which filled him caused him to levitate without his being able to control it.

One day Chögyam confessed to the hermit that he missed his parents, whom death had taken long before their time. The lama took advantage of the occasion to tell him about one of the most important teachings of Buddhism: the Four Noble Truths.

"Is your pain deep?" the lama asked.

Chögyam nodded.

"Then open your mind, Chögyam, since you have just realized for yourself the first Noble Truth which the Buddha taught us."

Chögyam frowned. "That death awaits us all?" he asked.

"No, but you're very close," the hermit acknowledged. "That all existence is suffering. Birth is suffering, and then all that follows after: illness, old age, death. There's no way to escape from suffering in the way man experiences his existence. Even the happy moments are no exception, as their unavoidably passing nature puts us in a state of permanent existential anxiety.

"I think I understand, master."

"Well, then understand the second Noble Truth: that the origin of suffering is desire. That's to say, the attachment we feel toward the objects we perceive through our senses, human passions, and the yearning for existence. And it's that desire for existence that leads us to perpetuate samsara, the eternal cycle of deaths and births."

Chögyam nodded several times, making efforts to understand, even though these Truths were beginning to seem too pessimistic to him.

"Wait until you hear the third Noble Truth, Chögyam," the hermit warned him, as if he had read the boy's mind. "The one which recognizes the cessation of suffering. What Buddha reveals is that once the cause of suffering has been determined, the suppression of it leads us to its end, and thereby to the attainment of true and definite happiness through Enlightenment."

"And what happens when you reach Enlightenment?"

"That cannot be described, you must feel it. But it would mean the absolute apprehension of wisdom, which would enable our spirit to perceive the true nature of both mind and reality. In any case, after attaining it we would finally interrupt the cycle of reincarnations."

"So, when someone reaches Awakening, they don't reincarnate anymore?"

"That's right," the lama confirmed. "Except the *bodhisattvas*, those great holy men who despite having attained Enlightenment decide to delay their entrance into Nirvana and are reincarnated once again, to contribute to the salvation of others through compassion. A bodhisattva of our time, for example, is the Karmapa, the leader of the Kagyu School."

"Is that why you came to this cave, master? To reach Enlightenment?"

"Yes, Chögyam."

"Have you reached it?"

The hermit smiled gently. "Not yet, but I'm beginning to feel I can touch it with my fingertips."

They remained silent for a long time, while Chögyam continued musing. "What is the fourth Noble Truth?"

"The fourth Noble Truth is the eightfold path. That is, the practices one must follow in order to cease suffering and attain Awakening. But that, Chögyam, I'll explain to you in more detail during the time you're with me."

At the end of spring the hermit informed Chögyam that he had something for him. The old man's eyes shone brightly and he was exhibiting the broad smile he showed so seldom. Chögyam was intrigued, for he did not know the reason for the mystery, nor could he imagine what his master might have in mind.

"Chögyam, I'm proud of you, of your efforts, and the progress you've made."

"Thank you, master."

"This is for you," he said, giving him something he had been hiding behind his back.

Chögyam looked at him, dazzled by the gift, which was as unexpected as it was picturesque. The hermit had carved the mythical figure of King Songtsen Gampo out of wood, in a martial stance, pulling back a bowstring on the point of releasing it.

"So that you can also play, since your training in dharma should cause no conflict with your inner being or cloud your child's soul."

Chögyam took the figure, which was the size of his hand, and admired it proudly. At that moment he wished he could have shown it to Thupten and shared games with his older brother.

"Master, do you really believe someone will ever come looking for me the way your vision showed you?"

"I'm sure of it," the hermit replied without hesitation. "But you don't need to worry about that. What's important is that when the time comes you should be ready."

Chögyam accepted the answer, although he found it hard to conceive why anyone would venture into those remote and barren mountains.

"May I go out and play with the warrior?"

The hermit gave him permission and followed Chögyam with his gaze. The boy soon disappeared among the boulders, letting his imagination soar as he went.

The lama hermit sighed in resignation. According to an ancient Buddhist saying, man must separate himself from everything he loves. A saying which he, more than anybody else, had followed to its ultimate consequences. Yet now, even though he had tried to avoid it, the affection he felt for that boy was shaking the foundations of his existence.

* * *

Kyentse Rinpoche and Tsultrim Trungpa reached the house they were looking for thanks to the directions the generous locals had given them.

"I never thought we'd be able to find it in such a maze of streets." Tsultrim panted.

"It wasn't that bad," Kyentse replied. "It's just that your fatigue from the journey has affected your sense of direction."

The two lamas were on the outskirts of the city of Shigatse, overwhelmed by the bustle of its neighborhoods, which contrasted so vividly with the peace they were used to at the monastery. Shigatse was southeast of Lhasa, about a hundred and sixty miles away. The journey had therefore been long and hard. It had taken them more than a week to reach their destination, and it had seemed like an eternity to them. But hope had been the engine that moved them to travel through the vast uplands and high plateaus which were typical of the inhospitable lands of Tibet, convinced that at last they would find the longed-for tulku.

Fifteen days before, they had received news at the Tsurphu Gompa of a new candidate. The omens were good, but before ringing the bells they sought consultation with the astrologers. And the results were encouraging. The readings, while not conclusive, strongly argued in favor of the candidate's authenticity. The usual procedure in such cases would have been to bring the presumptive candidate to the monastery to perform the relevant tests, but the euphoria Kyentse and Tsultrim felt was such that they decided to go and meet him themselves. It was so long since the death of the Karmapa, and there had been so many failed candidates, that they were confident their luck would have changed on this occasion.

Kyentse and Tsultrim had traveled with a merchant caravan which plied a commercial route with Nepal; it had traded in goods between the two nations since time immemorial. The merchants drove a pack of mules loaded with salt and Tibetan wool, which they would trade for rice and other cereals from the Nepalese lands. The two monks had made the journey on horseback, dressed in common clothes, so as to forestall any word of their arrival from reaching the candidate's family. Protocol demanded that they should present themselves without warning, to guarantee the legitimacy of the authorization process.

"Nervous?" Kyentse asked.

"More than you can imagine," Tsultrim admitted.

In front of them was the candidate's house. The walls were adobe and the roof made of straw. From its overall appearance they gathered it was a humble home, but not at all sunk in poverty.

At that moment they saw a small boy coming out of the house together with an older girl, who both disappeared rapidly round the corner. Kyentse and Tsultrim glanced at each other. This boy could very well be the tulku. Even better, this would allow them to approach the parents first, to tell them about the situation and make them aware of their intentions. The lamas walked toward the house.

The news which had reached Tsurphu spoke of the day the candidate was born. A cuckoo had landed on the roof and had not stopped singing all morning. In addition, the mother had reported having had a number of dreams during her pregnancy in which great bodhisattvas from the past enveloped her in a brilliant white light.

Kyentse and Tsultrim waited at the door until a middle-aged woman invited them to come in as soon as she noticed their presence. In Tibet, the doors of even the humblest home were always open to merchants or pilgrims in need of shelter. The lamas acknowledged the invitation by bowing their heads and followed her into her home.

The home had three rooms, and apart from a simple altar and a couple of shelves, there was no furniture. A rectangle of dim light came in through the only tiny window of the main room. Flies went in and out of the place and flew around undisturbed.

Kyentse and Tsultrim squatted on the floor and accepted the tea with butter that the woman hastily offered them. Although not the best they had had, the familiar taste comforted them after the rigors of the journey. In return for her hospitality, the lamas gave her a set of colorful silk scarves they had brought for the occasion. The head of the family greeted them with kindness and asked them about the reason for their visit. The monks did not beat about the bush. Tsultrim, as spokesman, revealed their true identities: he was the abbot of the Tsurphu Gompa and Kyentse Rinpoche had been the closest lama to the late Karmapa. And they were there to establish whether their son might be the reincarnation of the leader of the Kagyu School.

The couple, overwhelmed at the revelation, was unable to hide their joy. For a traditional Buddhist family like theirs there could be no greater honor than the recognition of a tulku among their children. The boy's name was Norbu, and he was five years old. The monks then asked to be told of the unusual events which had occurred in the boy's life. The mother explained the dreams she had had during her pregnancy, while the father told them about the episode of the singing bird which had taken place on the day of his birth. Afterward they went on to describe aspects of Norbu's personality and some of the more striking things he had said and done. The monks were satisfied and carefully summarized the current situation.

"For the moment, Norbu is just a candidate," Tsultrim said. "Now we're going to carry out a preliminary test. It won't be conclusive as yet, but if he passes it, the boy will come back with us to the monastery, as long as we have your consent, so that the last test can be carried out."

The couple nodded, not missing a word of what the two monks were explaining. Kyentse brought out a *mala* he was carrying with him and gave it to the woman.

"When Norbu arrives, offer it to him without saying a word," he said. "The rosary you hold in your hands belonged to the late Karmapa. We'll watch his reaction from the room next door, so that he doesn't know we're here."

"I will do this," she said.

"Then we'll come in and show ourselves to your son," Kyentse went on. "As you see, we're not dressed as monks, but if Norbu really is the reincarnated Karmapa he should recognize us, or at least show an open, positive attitude in our presence."

Norbu's parents agreed to collaborate in the plan put forward by the two monks disguised as merchants. Norbu and his older sister had gone to the market and would be back soon, so the head of the family stood outside to warn them as soon as he saw the children coming, giving Kyentse and Tsultrim enough time to hide.

The monks waited praying in front of the Buddha on the family altar. They did not wait long, and as soon as the father saw his children at the bottom of the street, they all ran to take up their positions.

The girl was the first to enter, laden with milk and butter, and her father indicated kindly that she should leave the things in the kitchen. The monks watched the scene from the shadows of the next room, peeping out from behind the curtain that served as a door. Then Norbu walked in, looking relaxed and bright-eyed. The boy took a couple of steps, then without any prompting prostrated himself before the altar with a deep fervor.

Kyentse and Tsultrim immediately felt very good vibrations.

Next the mother showed him the rosary exactly as she had been asked to do. Norbu looked at it closely and took it in his hands. He toyed with some of the beads, then after a minute hung it round his neck.

Tsultrim nudged Kyentse gently with his elbow, signaling the inward excitement he was suppressing. His bulging eyes seemed to want to burst out of their sockets. The monks exchanged a look that clearly expressed the joy they felt.

"Let's go outside," whispered the abbot.

From that moment on, everything went wrong.

The monks came out of their hiding place and showed themselves to Norbu, with gentle smiles on their kind faces. But the boy's reaction was far from what it should have been. Timidly, he hid behind his mother's legs. And when Kyentse went up to him quietly, he burst into tears at the presence of those strange men.

Disappointment was patent in the faces of both monks, and Norbu's parents knew at once that their son had not passed the preliminary test.

The true tulku would have to go on waiting somewhere, hoping to be found.

The journey back resembled a funeral. Kyentse and Tsultrim joined another caravan of Tibetan merchants coming from Nepal, following the same route in the opposite direction. They barely exchanged a word with the merchants or with each other. The weight of a new disappointment began to take its toll on the spirit of both lamas. The abbot, who was on the chubby side, lost some weight as a result of the strong emotions and harsh conditions of the journcy.

The way back seemed twice as long as the outward one. And when at last they arrived at the Tsurphu Monastery, a surprise awaited them which only served to increase the anxiety that gripped them: during their absence, a messenger had brought a letter to the gompa from their Buddhist brethren of the Sakya School.

Tsultrim read it without delay or ceremony, while Kyentse watched the changes in the abbot's face as he read further in the message. On the one hand they were told of the death of the Sakya leader, Sa'gya Pandita, who had taken upon himself the responsibility of introducing Prince Godan of the Mongols to the mysteries of the way of the dharma. And on the other, it was announced that the successor he had nominated was his own nephew Drogön Chögyal Phagpa, who at present was at the court of the Emperor Kublai Khan, sharing with him the teachings of the Buddha.

According to the letter, the Great Khan admitted that shamanic animism, the traditional Mongol religion, had ceased to be an effective solution that might help to give appropriate guidance to the spirituality of his people. In consequence, and thanks to the efforts of Drogön Chögyal Phagpa, he was considering the possibility of embracing Buddhism. But the emperor would not make a decision without first meeting the leader of the other great Tibetan Buddhist school, the Kagyu. In other words, he demanded to meet the Karmapa, something he would do as soon as his political obligations gave him a moment's respite.

The letter included a postscript: the Great Khan, who had been told about the peculiar system of succession followed by the Kagyu lineage, about which he had expressed certain reservations and considerable disbelief, would send a Mongol representative to supervise the authenticity of the selection process.

Kyentse and Tsultrim felt offended by the Emperor's insinuations, as they, more than anyone else, were the interested parties when it came to finding the genuine reincarnation of the Karmapa.

The problem now was that they might not do it in time.

CHAPTER IV

Summer

ཨོཾ་མུ་ནེ་མུ་ནེ་མ་ཧཱ་མུ་ནེ་ཨེ་སྭཱ་ཧཱ།

"The perfume of flowers does not go against the wind. Nor does that of sandalwood, or rose or jasmine. Yet the perfume of a virtuous man spreads everywhere and in all directions."

Dhammapada, 4-11

The end of spring coincided with the resounding failure of Wangchuk's plan, which, broadly speaking, took the form of getting Thupten to pass for a novice of the Batang Monastery, with the aim of fraudulently gaining food by exploiting the generosity of the Buddhist faithful.

The outlaw's blinding frustration faded as the days went by to the point when, after a cold analysis of the facts, Wangchuk was able to acknowledge his mistakes and the crudeness of his plan's execution. As a result, far from giving up his grotesque idea as Thupten would have wished, the outlaw busied himself in correcting its faults and putting it in practice again at the first opportunity. Hunger gnawed at his stomach, but stronger than that was the yearning to satisfy the call of alcohol, to which he had become addicted long ago.

Wangchuk found out that the bowl the monks used could not be made of wood, so he traded the one he had for one of clay. As for clothes, he took far more care to dye them the correct color and even took the trouble to perfume them with the essence of wild flowers. Finally and to Thupten's chagrin, as his hair had grown again since the last bloodbath, the boy had to go through a new torture which seemed, if such a thing were possible, even bloodier than the first. This time at least Wangchuk muttered an apology, declaring that with only one hand and the stump of the other his skills as a barber were limited.

Coinciding with the arrival of summer, the outlaw made full preparations for putting his plan into practice once again, calculated now to the last detail. This time he could not fail. Even the house had not been chosen at random; far from it. Wangchuk had noticed the high level of generosity showed by its owners toward the demands of the Buddhist monks. So without more ado Thupten took his place in front of the door, and Wangchuk hid in an alley so that he could watch events unfold without being seen.

Not a moment had passed when Thupten heard the outlaw calling from his hiding place and making exaggerated gestures at him. The boy did not understand, but everything seemed to indicate that he was warning him about something. An instant later, Thupten felt a hand on his shoulder. He turned. A Buddhist monk was staring down at him, a real one, unlike Thupten himself, who only hoped to be taken for one thanks to a stolen bowl and a habit made from patches.

Thupten swallowed hard and prepared for the scolding that was surely on its way.

"You don't belong to the order," the monk said, gazing at Thupten with a grimace of repulsion on his face.

It was not until he raised his head and looked into the monk's eyes that Thupten recognized the voyeur he had surprised at the river when he had followed the outlaw through the trees. Other Buddhist monks appeared and joined their leader. Thupten turned his glance toward Wangchuk. The outlaw was still there, tucked away in the alley and watching the scene at a safe distance.

Lama Dechen touched the material of Thupten's clothing as if he wanted to be even more certain about the imposture. "Who are you and what are you doing here?" he asked in a threatening voice.

Thupten lowered his head and fixed his eyes on the ground. He'd better keep his mouth shut.

The old lama nodded slowly, soon realizing the boy would not say a single word.

The monks who were accompanying Dechen asked him what he was thinking of doing with the boy.

"He's a usurper. I'll take him to the authorities so that he gets what he deserves."

Lama Dechen grabbed Thupten's arm and dragged him down the street. The boy did not resist, as that would only make his situation worse. But then, before he had even advanced a dozen yards, he felt someone had grabbed his other arm and was pulling him in the opposite direction, forcing Dechen to stop. At that moment Thupten looked like a toy that two children were fighting over.

Thupten's surprise grew even greater when he saw that the other contender was… a woman. More than that… a Buddhist nun!

Dechen glared at Tenzin, but the abbess of the convent of the bhikkhuni, though small in size, was not prepared to be intimidated.

"What are you intending to do?" she said. "Don't you see he's just a boy?"

"He's committed a crime, and that's what matters," Dechen retorted. "The rest is for the authorities to decide."

"But don't you know what they'll do to him?" she insisted. "Or don't you care?"

Dechen shrugged, a gesture which showed perfectly just how little he cared about the boy's fate.

Thupten felt that at this point his opinion deserved to be considered. "I'll get told off," he said with apparent ease, not knowing why they were making such a big fuss over such a small matter. "But that's all."

Tenzin put her hands to her head. It did not take a genius to realize the boy had been duped by some unscrupulous rogue who must be using him for his own benefit. "What's your name?" she asked warmly.

Thupten told her. The Buddhist nun bent over him and raised his chin so gently, barely touching his skin, that he was reminded of his mother, whose soft touch he had thought forgotten forever.

"Thupten, if they take you to the authorities, they'll cut your hand off, if not both of them," she said.

The news was like a hammer blow that left him breathless. A knot formed in his throat, and for an instant he nearly lost control of his sphincters. Instinctively he looked for Wangchuk, naively hoping the outlaw would come to his rescue like a heroic champion. But Wangchuk had vanished some time before: as soon as he realized things were turning serious.

Tenzin turned to Dechen, putting into each of the words she spoke all the feeling she could muster. "Take pity on the boy and let him go. I beg you from the bottom of my heart."

The old lama looked at her for a while before he answered, perhaps keen to savor his reply to the full. "Your pleading doesn't inspire the least compassion in me," he blurted out. "In any case, distrust. Even though you're a Buddhist nun you're a woman first and foremost, and it's precisely your sensitive nature which makes you incapable of following the strict rules of religious discipline. This case, in fact, is proof of it."

Tenzin looked for support among the monks who had come with Dechen, but as they were all disciples of his, none of them dared oppose him.

"The boy is coming with me, and he'll get his just punishment," Dechen declared. "That's my last word."

This said, he dragged the boy again. This time Thupten struggled with the old lama, trying to free himself from his grasp. Dechen, unmoved, used all the strength he considered necessary to bring him under control, even at the risk of hurting the boy.

Suddenly a powerful voice echoed behind them, putting an end to the scuffle. "What's going on here?"

Thupten turned round and was impressed by the big Buddhist monk who had appeared on the scene. He was taller than his own father, who up till now had been the tallest man he had ever known. Lobsang Geshe, arms akimbo, stared impatiently at all of them in turn.

"He's a usurper and he's broken the law," Dechen explained. And boasting, he added, "I found him myself."

"Please, Lobsang," Tenzin cut in, on the brink of tears. "Don't let him take him."

Lobsang looked into the boy's eyes, in which as well as fear he sensed a deep sadness. Time seemed to expand while the abbot puzzled over the best solution. He wanted to save the boy, but it was not going to be easy. Dechen knew he had him on the ropes, because the law was on his side.

"Let him go," he said at last. "We won't turn him in."

Dechen's face lengthened until it reached an extreme of disbelief. "What are you talking about?" he cried. "You can't cover up an offense like this. I'm warning you, if you don't report him according to your duty, you automatically become his accomplice."

"Nobody's going to report him, because as of this moment he's one of ours," said Lobsang. "I've resolved to take him as my personal disciple. From now on, I'll be his tutor and I'll guide him through the way of dharma for the rest of his long life."

From Dechen's throat came a sound that was half a curse and half a frustrated laugh. "This is ridiculous," he objected. "Besides, in the ten years you've been in Batang you've never had a disciple of your own."

"Then it's high time I had one."

Thupten listened to the debate, overwhelmed by what was happening. He guessed that the big monk, who seemed to be important, had saved him from a horrible fate. But he was still very confused about how the conflict was going to be resolved.

"The boy's name is Thupten," Tenzin said, smiling from ear to ear.

"Shut up," retorted Dechen, who in spite of everything was not yet prepared to give up. "The boy's too young to enter the monastery," he argued in desperation.

"Of course, but not too young to stop him being maimed for life, eh?" Tenzin replied with sarcasm.

"Settle down," Lobsang said. "How old are you, Thupten?"

Apart from being healthy, the Vinaya only stipulated that the novice had to be old enough to scare a crow away.

Thupten mastered his nerves and replied as best he could. "The last time I was six, sir. But lately I've lost count."

"That seems enough for me," said Lobsang. "And now come with me, we have a lot to talk about."

On the way to the monastery, Thupten told Lobsang about the terrible tragedy his family had been victim of when they were crossing the mountain pass just before Batang. He went on to tell him about his encounter with the outlaw, his activities as a beggar, and the painful conditions he had suffered during the past six months, including the abuse and malnutrition.

Lobsang listened in silence without interrupting him at all, overwhelmed by the bitter account coming out of the boy's mouth. When he had finished, the abbot was sure that he had made the right decision and that, given the circumstances, entering the monastery as a novice was the best thing that could happen to Thupten.

The boy never mentioned the name of the outlaw or any other piece of information which could lead to his identification, not only because he was still terrified of him but also because he had not yet accepted the fact that he was free of the man for good. In fact, as soon as they left the city limits Thupten kept looking everywhere, thinking that Wangchuk would suddenly appear, attack the Buddhist monk, and take him away again as if the boy were an animal he owned.

"Thupten, you must know that the commitment I have taken upon me in offering to be your tutor is highly valued among us. In exchange, all I ask of you is to make the noble effort to become a Buddhist monk some day."

Thupten did not answer immediately, not because he disagreed with Lobsang but for a much more prosaic reason, which made him deeply ashamed. "Lama Lobsang, I'm not saying no, and I'm even looking forward to it," he whispered, his head bent. "But I'm telling you, all I know about Buddhism is just the name, and until recently I didn't even know it existed. In the village where I used to live no Buddhist monk ever came to teach us, and here in Batang I watched you all from afar, but the man who kept me never wanted to tell me anything." The boy looked up, embarrassed of his confession. What if Lobsang was angry with him because of his unpardonable ignorance?

The abbot looked at him for a long time, open-mouthed, then burst into a loud guffaw. He could not remember the last time he had laughed so heartily. "You needn't worry about that," he said as soon as he recovered his composure. "We'll see that you learn the philosophy and the teachings of the Buddha, the rules and habits of monastic life, and good behavior as well."

Thupten sighed with relief, feeling a great load had been taken off his shoulders.

"However, it won't be an easy path either," Lobsang said. "When you're ordained as a monk, you'll have to follow two hundred and twenty-seven rules."

Although Thupten did not know that figure, he guessed it must be very big. A sudden change in his expression showed his bewilderment.

"And what will happen to me if I break any of the rules?"

"Don't be alarmed, Thupten; everything has a solution. Most faults, depending on their type, entail their own penance, either repentance or simple confession. Only faults in the category of *parajika*, the most serious, entail expulsion from the monastery."

"And what are those?" the boy asked with great interest.

"All right, as you want to know them, I'll tell you," Lobsang said. "Although, believe me, you're too young still for them to affect you. The first one punishes sexual interaction, and don't ask me to explain because your time for it hasn't come yet. The second refers to stealing, to be exact anything with a value of at least one twenty-fourth part of an ounce of gold. The third condemns the act of killing, that's to say, intentionally taking somebody's life. And the fourth and last one sanctions the monk who deliberately lies to someone else about having reached states of superior awareness."

On hearing those words Thupten stopped dead, covered his face with his hands, and threw himself on the ground, sobbing desperately.

This unexpected reaction confused Lobsang so much that he was frozen to the spot. Then he picked the boy up and while he did his best to console him, wiped his cheeks, which were stained with the dirty marks of tears. "What's the matter?"

Thupten then described, between hiccups and sobs, the events that had led him first to steal in the market and later to kill a street dog. More than enough reasons, Thupten believed, according to all those rules, to be excluded for life from the peaceful Buddhist community. Lobsang put his arm around the boy and comforted him with a solemn caress. He needed to be given affection, trust, and safety, emotions that he seemed to have forgotten while he had been under the influence of the outlaw.

"But you were forced to do it, weren't you?" he argued. "In that case it doesn't count. Leave all that behind and focus on what awaits you in your new life. As soon as we get to the monastery you'll feel that you're part of a big family."

Lobsang's words were effective. Thupten recovered at once, and they went on with the sole company of the morning sun and the clammy dryness of the atmosphere.

Half an hour with the boy had been enough to impress Lobsang with the enormous honesty of Thupten's small but great heart.

As they neared the monastery, there loomed into Thupten's view the first prayer banners which told the visitor the Buddhist sanctuary was near. Countless strings of rectangular flags hung horizontally from long cords fastened to rocks and trees, somehow decorating nature itself with a festive, multicolored quality that nobody could have missed.

Lobsang stopped and showed him one from up close. "Look carefully," he said. "The flags carry sacred formulas which the wind captures with its wayward breath, then spreads among all those who, like us, walk the path leading to the monastery."

Soon these flags were joined by others, much bigger this time, hanging from wooden poles several feet tall, which flanked the path like sentinels from an imperial court. Thupten saw the formidable standards waving and could not help feeling they were there to welcome him.

Presently they came across the first monks wandering in the area round the monastery. Some of them carried a cylinder with a wooden handle which they turned endlessly.

"They're prayer mills," Lobsang told him. He had not failed to notice the boy's sudden interest. "The inside is filled with mantras written on strips of paper whose blessings are scattered through the air like the rings that spread across a pool after you throw a stone onto the surface."

Thupten had paid good attention to Lobsang's explanations, but what he really wanted was to try one for himself. The abbot asked a passing monk for his mill and gave it to the boy to have temporarily. Thupten took it in earnest and straight away began to make it twirl frantically, while a smile of pure happiness appeared on his face. Lobsang was fully aware that the boy was using the mill as if it were a toy instead of a sacred object, but he was not upset: his first task must consist of giving Thupten's lost joy back to him, after it had been taken away by blows and threats.

The group of monastic buildings, put up by Lobsang during the last decade, a small citadel of knowledge and meditation, appeared in front of them like a castle in a fairy tale, set in the middle of a majestic valley. In the foreground was the temple and behind it the other structures that surrounded it: the monks' residence, the school for novices, and the library, all at its back, as if they meant to protect it.

They went through into the precinct and crossed the lovingly tended garden which lined the perimeter at the front. Already many monks had gathered there. Most greeted Lobsang with a bow and the palms of their hands brought together at chin level. Thupten looked at everything with eyes filled with curiosity and, for the first time since the loss of his family, with hope. An original ornament that crowned the roof, right on the edge, caught his attention. "What is it?"

"It's the wheel of dharma, which symbolizes the teachings of the Buddha. As you can see, it's flanked by two deer contemplating it with devotion. Buddha began to preach his doctrine in the Deer Park of Sarnath, so that by representing these animals we aim to commemorate that precious instant."

"Could we visit that park, Lama Lobsang?"

"I'm afraid not, Thupten. It's a very long way from here, so much so that it's not even in Tibet but in India."

A golden gable pointing at the sky topped the cusp of the sloping roof. Lobsang dreamed of covering the whole roof in gold, as well as the dharma wheel. That display of riches was not seen as such from the Buddhist perspective, since gold, far from being only an esthetic decoration, served an eminently divine function.

An extraordinary and colorful fresco adorned the outside of the northern wall of the temple. The functional illiteracy of the majority of population, with the exception of the monastic community and the wealthier classes, demanded a profusion of illustrations and carvings whose educational function was not just fascinating but fundamental. It took Thupten less than a second to feel attracted to the painting that took up the entire width of the wall and in which, in spite of its magnificence, the artist had not renounced to portray the most insignificant details. The contents of the painting were a jumble as far as Thupten was concerned, but the beings that composed it—from men and animals to gods, demonic creatures and others harder to categorize—seemed to have a life of their own.

"What you see is the representation of the wheel of existences," Lobsang was prompted to tell him. "The samsara to which we're all subject."

"Why are those animals in the center?"

"They incarnate the three poisons: the pig represents ignorance; the rooster, desire; and the snake, anger and hatred. The three poisons are the internal engines which make the wheel turn and hold man captive in the samsara. To fight them, you'll have to acquire the two principal qualities of a monk: wisdom and compassion."

The different worlds, more or less painful, were represented in turn around a large concentric circle, in which the beings could be born again according to their karma. Thupten pointed, almost fearful, at a terrifying monster which seemed to be biting the wheel fiercely.

"That is Yama, the God of Death," Lobsang explained. "He holds the wheel with his fangs and also his claws, and at the same time he rules pitilessly over all beings in the samsara."

"And how do you leave the wheel?" Thupten asked.

"When you reach Enlightenment, as the Buddha himself did."

Thupten was enjoying Lobsang's explanations as well as his gentle but powerful voice. It was nice to receive warm words instead of beatings for a change.

"Would you like to see inside the temple?"

Thupten nodded enthusiastically; he did not need to be told twice.

At that moment Dorjee appeared. At a sign from Lobsang, he came up to them, deeply intrigued by the boy's presence. The young monk did not hide his surprise when he heard Lobsang tell him that he had taken the boy as a disciple.

"If only I could have been that lucky!" he joked affectionately.

"You mustn't exaggerate," Lobsang replied, "although I appreciate the compliment. You can't have done so badly when you're about to reach the level of lama. Very soon you'll turn into the youngest lama in your own right in the Batang Monastery." Then Lobsang whispered something in Dorjee's ear, and the young man left to go somewhere else, not without first quickly glancing at Thupten.

When they went in through the doors of the temple, the boy's eyes needed to adapt to the reigning darkness within, which contrasted with the burning brightness outside. After this brief lapse of time, the shadowy curtain woven by the lamps of yak butter allowed him to make out an explosion of forms and colors which took him completely by surprise.

The room was filled with frescoes, statues, and ornaments, distributed around the walls and the altar so that there was not an empty space in sight. The Tibetans, condemned to populate the barren lands of the top of the world and accustomed to living a rough and demanding existence, compensated by pouring into their divine halls all the luxuries and exuberance lacking in their humdrum routine. Thupten felt the hair on his arms stand on end. The place exuded peace, but within it was also a mysterious undercurrent, charged with such powerful energy that he could feel it by extending his hands in front of his face.

Thupten fixed his gaze on several monks who were seated on cushions, praying in deep concentration while their hands swayed from side to side, shaping different gestures in a rapid sequence. The scene immediately reminded him of that strange Buddhist monk who had faced night in the graveyard by himself. Thupten moved his hands without realizing, as if they did of their own accord, trying to imitate the complex activity.

"These gestures of the hands are called *mudras*," said Lobsang, "and each one of them has a different meaning. In this case they represent offerings. For example, when they put their hands together like a cup, they are offering water. But if they place their fingers one on top of another as if they were smoke spiraling upward, then the offering is of incense. And usually, between one mudra and the next they make a graceful circle."

Thupten took a couple of steps forward and looked around him. He did not see a single corner without paintings. The walls which the faithful leaned against during great meetings were painted purplish-red to hip level, whereas the rest, the whole upper part, was completely covered with frescoes representing the great divinities, like Avalokiteshvara, Tera, or Manyushri. From the ceiling, blue in allusion to the sky, hung cylindrical streamers made of rows of little ribbons with rhomboid ends. Some corners of the covering, on the other hand, showed grey spots which spoiled the whole, caused by the perennial smoke of the many lard candles.

The throne dominating the hall caught Thupten's attention. Excitedly and without stopping to consider the sacred character of the place, he ran up to it, passing through the rows of monks and stepping on them here and there in his impetuous gallop. Lobsang was quick to excuse him, calling on their understanding and patience. The throne, covered in brocade and completed with an imposing back support, faced the audience and was reserved for the highest-ranking representative. This honor usually fell to Lobsang, except when he was traveling, in which case Lama Dechen took his place.

"May I sit on it?" Thupten asked.

Lobsang was surprised by the boy's incredible boldness, since no other novice would even have thought of asking such a thing, supremely improper and out of place. Yet he made no objection. Lobsang had decided that Thupten's first day at the monastery should be unlike any other he had had in a long time. "All right. But just this once," he conceded.

Thupten climbed onto the throne as if he had done it all his life, and from there he looked on the scene with a broad smile and a glow in his eyes that Lobsang would never forget.

"Now you must come down," he urged after a while.

Thupten complied and turned his steps toward the altar, his interest in everything he saw undiminished.

The altar was made of a set of large shelves, divided into compartments on several levels, whose place of honor (as could hardly be otherwise) was reserved for a statue of the Buddha. In the western world the presence of the altar is directly related to the idea of sacrifice, whereas in the Buddhist tradition, by contrast, it is associated with that of offering. The statue, golden as fire, was disproportionately large in comparison with the rest of the objects on the altar.

Lobsang made three prostrations, which Thupten watched curiously. Then, without any prompting or giving any warning, he did the same in imitation of his master: more clumsily than otherwise, but with a determination which many other novices far better prepared than he was himself might have envied. Lobsang judged Thupten's spontaneity to be a positive thing, even though he was sure it would be hard for him to make it fit in with the tightly restricted monastic life.

Thupten scratched his head at the presence of a series of bowls, perfectly aligned and separated from one another by no more than a finger's width.

"They're the offering bowls," Lobsang said. "Essential on any self-respecting altar."

"And what's this?" Thupten asked pointing at several strange conical figurines which bore no resemblance to anything he had ever seen before.

"They're *tormas*, another type of offering, made from lard and flour, destined both to attract the blessing of the divinities and to placate the adverse forces. But don't let the idea of eating them enter your head!" said Lobsang, who had already had warning of the boy's sudden impulses.

Thupten gave an exaggerated grimace, jokingly, as if Lobsang had broken his heart. At that moment someone opened the doors of the temple and a beam of natural light spread through the hall. It was Dorjee, returning from the errand Lobsang had sent him on a few minutes before. The young monk closed the door behind him and came up to them.

"Thank you," Lobsang said, taking the things Dorjee had brought.

Thupten tried to discover what these objects were, like a dog sniffing the top of a table. It did not take him long to find out. The things were for him.

"Here." Lobsang handed them to him. "It's time you got rid of what you're wearing and put on clothes worthy of a Buddhist monk."

Thupten admired the robe with utter disbelief. It was clean, it smelt good and what was more important still, he could wear it without being accused of fraud.

"And here's your alms bowl," said Lobsang. "Take good care of it and no matter what happens, never lose sight of it."

Thupten gripped the bowl as if he feared that at the last minute the Buddhist monks would regret having taken him in.

"Now I'll show you your room," Lobsang announced.

"Does it have a roof?"

Lobsang and Dorjee exchanged glances, and were unable to keep from laughing despite the looks of reproach from the rest of the monks, whose meditation they had interrupted.

"It has a roof and even a bed. Come on, we'll leave the temple and you can see it for yourself."

Thupten followed them, for the first time in months feeling blessed with happiness.

He had not been two weeks in the monastery, and Thupten was already going to take part in one of the most important rituals of

Theravada Buddhism. It was the usual act of Uposatha, exclusively for monks and lamas, but once a year, with the aim of strengthening the spirit of unity of the whole monastic community of Batang, Lobsang allowed both the novices and the bhikkhuni nuns to attend. He was even planning to permit the presence of the lay faithful in the future, with the aim of renewing the commitment on the part of all the parties involved to watch over the spiritual wellbeing of the whole of society, and keep the teachings of the Buddha alive.

Until that moment, Thupten's first days at the monastery could not have been better. He was learning to read and write in the school of novices, even though he was finding it a nightmare to get used to that jumble of squiggles they called the alphabet, which until then he had never heard about. He was also being instructed in the teachings of the Buddha, whose philosophy they approached in a simple way for even the smallest children to understand. Finally, he had begun to memorize his first sutra, which very soon he would have to recite in front of the whole class.

Besides, Thupten had already been given his first task— always assigned to the youngest—which involved serving the classic tea with butter to those monks who were celebrating a long ceremony. Thupten would then go through the ordered rows of monks, laden with a smoking metal container. It was so heavy when it was filled that when he dragged it beside him, it almost made him lose his balance.

At night, Thupten relived his comfortless days with the outlaw in all kinds of sinister nightmares; because of this he was grateful he shared a room with other novices, whose simple presence to a large extent calmed his fear of falling asleep. For the same reason, his worst times were when he had to move through town begging for food among the faithful. There, outside the walls of the monastery, he felt vulnerable again and imagined Wangchuk's eyes on the back of his neck, stalking him silently, waiting for some opportunity to seize him from the hands of the Buddhist monks.

The time he had spent with the outlaw had deeply upset his personality and produced certain psychological aftereffects. Thupten dealt freely with the other children who lived in the monastery, but not so with the adults, whom he could not avoid regarding distrustfully as a result of his traumatic experience with Wangchuk. Of course he knew that the monks wished him no harm, but the seed of distrust was so deeply implanted that it could only be hoped its effects would fade with time. The only one who escaped Thupten's critical eye—and it could hardly be otherwise, since apart from being his teacher he had saved his life—was Lobsang. With him he was sociable and open, like the chatterbox he had always been.

Even so, there was one monk who, Thupten's grudges aside, did look upon the boy with open dislike, as if his presence in the community devalued it or implied a personal outrage. Because of this, whenever possible Thupten tried to avoid Lama Dechen, although there were times such as when he had to serve him tea when it was impossible to get away from his reproachful, accusing look.

For Dechen, the boy's admission to the order was the straw that broke the camel's back. Lobsang's willful decision implied not only excusing criminal behavior, but also taking away his authority before Tenzin, who once again had come out victorious. Dechen had not stopped turning things over in his mind lately, and there was so much spite in him that he had resolved to take the matter into his own hands in the most drastic way possible: once the Uposatha ceremony had finished, the old lama would go into the city and report Thupten as an impostor—a crime especially repudiated by both society and the Buddhist order—and report Lobsang too for covering up such a heinous crime. The facts were indisputable, quite apart from the fact that Dechen could count on several witnesses, his own disciples, who would testify to the truth of the accusation as well as anything else he chose to write in his report. He could not have cared less about the boy's fate, but he did care about what would happen to Lobsang. After the overwhelming scandal, the official authorities would not hesitate to bring the full force of the law down on him and condemn him accordingly. As a result Lobsang would lose his position as a monk and therefore as abbot, a post which Dechen would hurry to take on himself, not so much for his own good as for the whole community, which at a difficult moment like this would need a firm and experienced leader like himself.

On the morning of the ceremony, the golden gable that crowned the roof of the temple shone with penetrating flashes of fire, borrowed from a relentless sun which in the course of the day would gradually hide itself shyly behind the mountains that sheltered the monastery.

The bhikkhuni arrived together in perfect harmony, twirling their prayer mills, making use of their maras to pray, and harboring within them an overflowing joy. It was no wonder: Lobsang was offering them an opportunity to share in the Uposatha together with the male order, which for the nuns meant both a way of legitimizing themselves and an element of sincere support in the heart of a deeply male chauvinist society. The event also held special significance for the novices, as it represented a unique chance to familiarize themselves with a ritual in which they would take an active part when they were ordained as monks.

To avoid problems of space the ceremony would take place outside, with the garden as a stage and the good weather as a traveling companion. They all stood in rows one above the other, the monks on one side and the bhikkhuni and novices opposite them, like two armies facing each other in the battlefield, both sides separated by an improvised altar on which the usual offerings had been placed.

Shortly before the ceremony began, Tenzin spoke briefly with Lobsang in a relaxed atmosphere. Apart from exchanging courteous greetings, Lobsang only had time to show his interest in the progress of the building of the convent in Litang, and Tenzin to thank him for his invitation to a ceremony which held so much value for the bhikkhuni. Afterward the leader of the nuns' convent went to the place assigned to her, smiling warmly at Thupten, whom she saw happily placed nearby, crowded among the youngest novices.

Thupten did not feel nervous as much as intrigued. Both Lobsang and his schoolteachers had told him about the importance of that ceremony, something that even the oldest novices had confirmed. Thupten had never seen all the monks and novices of the monastery together before, and that sight alone was enough to impress him. He was glad to see the bhikkhuni too and did not hesitate to smile back at the nun who had defended him when nobody else had until Lobsang's miraculous appearance.

The ceremony, according to protocol, should have been led by Lobsang, or in his stead any of the other lamas living at the monastery. But this time the abbot decided to make an exception to the rule and pass the torch to Dorjee, who although not yet formally a lama, had already passed all the relevant tests with excellent marks, including the Chöd ritual he had performed the previous spring. Dorjee thanked Lobsang for the invitation, and in spite of the responsibility it involved, it never occurred to him to reject such an honor.

Meanwhile Dechen watched with disgust the grotesque mockery which had been made of the ceremony, even if it was only once a year, what with the unjustifiable presence of the bhikkhuni and the novices, and to crown it all, presided over by a monk who had not even reached the rank of lama. This was simply one more eccentricity on the part of Lobsang, who when it suited him was happy to ignore those rules he was not interested in. At least it all gave him further reason to back up his decision; he would make the accusation as soon as the ceremony was over. Lobsang's hours as abbot, Dechen told himself, were numbered.

At last everybody was in their places. The voices dropped to whispers and the whispers to silence. Dorjee breathed in deeply and turned to the attendants to begin the ceremony with the usual proclamation, "Let the community listen to me, venerable people, today is the day of Uposatha, the fifteenth of the fifteen. Let the ritual commence."

To begin with, the group of musician monks played their instruments. The singing monks joined in the melody, intoning a mantra of welcome in perfect unison. The symphony of sounds spread through the place as the tide submerges the beach, radiating through the atmosphere and making Thupten's soul vibrate like nothing else in the world, since he had never had the chance to witness the polyphonic arts of the monks who specialized in music.

The cymbals led the music with their gentle tinkling, followed an instant later by the rhythmical beat of the drums, played energetically by young monks who waved their drumsticks in a wide circle before every beat. The horns, as big as telescopes and more than six feet long, were played in pairs, producing a powerful braying that Thupten associated with the yawning of the depths of the Earth. The orchestra was completed by the *kangling*, a type of flute carved in bone from a human femur, which produced a prolonged echo stopped at the player's will, together with the long lament of the conch, whose sound faded in the middle of the concert like the call to retreat of a defeated battalion.

114

The deep voices of the monks, perfectly integrated with the music, were also exceptional, as from a basis of guttural sounds they reached impossible frequencies, managing at the same time to produce a note which was both tonal and perfectly harmonious.

The music stopped, leaving the trail of its magical echoes behind in the particles of the air. Immediately afterward Dorjee spoke once again, initiating a mantra in which all joined, whose end was to transform the offerings placed on the altar into their corresponding spiritual and allegorical forms.

Next, he came to the part which made up the essential core of the ceremony. "Whoever has committed a fault, let him declare it. Whoever has not, let him be silent. From your silence, venerable people, I shall know that you are pure."

Dorjee went on to recite the different rules of the disciplinary code, divided into groups relating to attire, food, private property, and various other aspects, after which some monks—and nuns as well—stood up to acknowledge their faults, receiving the corresponding penance when appropriate, direct absolution in other cases. Everything followed its usual course.

Finally Dorjee began to read the last set of rules, the faults under the category of parajika, whose disobedience was punished with immediate expulsion. Of course nobody expected anybody to come forward, since such cases were truly exceptional, and in the last decade, for example, they could have been counted on the fingers of one hand. Nevertheless, Dorjee waited for the allotted time, which, as it could hardly fail to be, was filled with a sepulchral silence.

Until, to everybody's surprise, it was interrupted by the sobbing of a young nun.

All those present fixed their gaze on the bhikkhuni, astonished by her unusual reaction. Dorjee wished from the bottom of his heart that he would not be obliged to record a disqualification in his first ceremony as a celebrant, much less that of a nun. In any case, he could not make any decision without first listening to whatever she had to say, something everyone was now awaiting expectantly.

But as time went by without the protagonist giving any indication of quenching her sobs or regaining control over herself, Tenzin came to her help and to give her support in this delicate situation. The abbess's embrace gradually had its effect, and the nun recovered her composure. However, given her obvious inability to speak in public, she opted for sharing with Tenzin, whispering in her ear, the thoughts which afflicted her so much.

Tenzin's face took on a hieratic poise few had seen before, and she took a step forward so firmly that more than one of those present began to swallow hard. Dorjee gave her permission to speak, hoping that in this way all doubts could be resolved.

"I beg you to excuse Bhasundara. Her nervousness prevents her from speaking out loud, so that I shall pass on the confidence she has just revealed to me, and of which none of us nuns had knowledge of till this moment." Tenzin's gaze radiated indignation, and at the same time deep disappointment. "She says that a few days ago, while she was bathing in the river behind our convent, she saw a man spying on her, hidden in the undergrowth. A person whom, by his robes, she identified unmistakably as a Buddhist monk."

The words fell on the monks like a jug of cold, or rather poisoned, water.

"And that's not all," announced Tenzin, determined not to omit any detail, no matter how suggestive. "The person in question apparently was not content merely to watch, but was satisfying his sexual instincts by succumbing to the pleasures of onanism."

An endless babble of comments burst out among the monks, who were cautious by nature, making it abundantly clear that very few gave any credit to that wild story. When they looked at each other they all knew themselves to be innocent, and it was hard for them to admit that one of their own might have behaved in such a puerile manner. Meanwhile Dechen looked elsewhere, as if it had nothing to do with him.

The matter had taken on such importance that Lobsang, who until that moment had stayed on the edge of things, now assumed the leadership which was his by rank.

"Silence, please," he begged, spreading arms wide. Then, raising his voice, he went on, "Tenzin, Bhasundara's accusation is extremely serious, but without specifying who it was, it serves for little or nothing except to stir up the entire congregation. It would therefore be a great help if Bhasundara could recognize the monk in question amongst us."

Tenzin nodded and exchanged a few words with Bhasundara, who continued sobbing amid a huddle of sympathetic nuns. The abbess then passed on once again what the nun had told her privately.

"Bhasundara was hoping from the bottom of her heart that the monk would have already confessed his fault; that's why she broke down in tears when she realized he wasn't going to. And although she could point out the culprit without any question of doubt, having to do so terrifies her and she begs that you won't put her in such a difficult situation."

"I see…" said Lobsang.

"On a personal level," Tenzin added, "I would like to state that if Bhasundara tells a story like this it's because it actually happened. And I want everyone to know that I trust her completely."

Tenzin's words, far from quieting tempers, fanned the flames of indignation still further, since until they got to the bottom of the matter the shadow of doubt would remain hovering over each and every one of the monks, with no distinction.

Lobsang was forced to beg for calm once more, and his voice reached every corner of the monastery.

"I give the offender my guarantee that if he confesses his fault now, I'll give him a new opportunity he doesn't even deserve. But if he remains silent and stays hidden, then he'll have me to face, because what is even worse than the fault he's accused of is the lie, since that hurts not only himself but the entire community."

A dense silence, thick as a curtain of incense, took hold of the place. Lobsang swept his gaze over the monks for whom he had done so much, but none of them returned any gesture that suggested guilt. A priori, all the faces, without exception, seemed to reflect nothing but the tenseness of the moment. Lobsang wanted to avoid pressing the nun as far as he possibly could, but if nobody confessed, he would have to.

At that point Lobsang felt someone tugging at his sleeve. He turned and looked down. Who should be there but Thupten, who had come all the way around the garden going behind the monks and novices and was standing at his side unnoticed.

"Not now, Thupten," he chided. "Please go back to your place."

But instead of that, Thupten pointed at Dechen and proclaimed in a loud voice, "It was him. I saw him too."

A muffled outcry followed Thupten's revelation, then a few seconds of unbearable tension. Dechen feigned surprise but lost neither his nerve nor his composure. If he gave way to anger he would only lend credit to the boy's words and come down to his level, so he worked out a reply which would show him at the same time firm in content and elegant in expression. The old lama knew perfectly well what role to play.

"Lobsang, you should control your pupil better. He probably thinks this is just a game, and he wants to take part in it. But quite apart from your deficiencies as a tutor, which have been made plain today, those you possess as abbot are even worse. Because with your brilliant ideas, along with all their weight of originality and good intentions, you've managed to turn one of the most solemn ceremonies of our order into a drama worthy of the best theatre in town. None of this is serious, Lobsang. To begin with, because neither novices nor bhikkhuni should be present in the ceremony of Uposatha."

Dechen's staging had been perfect. He had barely bothered to refute the accusation and instead had turned on Lobsang and his more unorthodox decisions in order to deflect attention from the real problem.

But Lobsang, far from being fooled by Dechen's oratory and his apparent calm, bent over and asked Thupten to explain why he had made a statement like that. For several minutes they talked in whispers before the uneasy gaze of those present, who watched what was happening and waited for more to be revealed. Thupten gave Lobsang a blow-by-blow account of the episode of the outlaw by the river, and he did it with such detail that the abbot ruled out any possibility of an ingenious lie, still more because he knew that honesty, with capital letters, was an unshakeable part of Thupten's nature.

Lobsang stood up and turned to Dechen, taking up the conflict where they had left it. "I believe the boy is telling the truth," he said. "I haven't the slightest doubt of it. What's more, Thupten saw you in the spring, so I'd guess this wasn't the first time."

Dechen gritted his teeth, unable to hide the color that was rising in his cheeks. His impassive façade was beginning to crack with every successive blow. "It's unbelievable that you should give more credit to a boy than to a lama. But coming from you, by now nothing would surprise me." Dechen was bearing up well. He went on playing his hand with the skill of an expert gambler.

"The novice isn't lying!" Bhasundara cried out suddenly. The nun, at last spurred on by the boy's courage, gathered enough of her own to make a public accusation of a lama whose influence and power had been enough to scare her without him speaking a single word. "I'm sorry I didn't say it right at the start, but indeed, it's Lama Dechen who was spying on me."

Bhasundara's confession caused great commotion. The monks moved restlessly in their places, prodding each other with their elbows and muttering astonished comments. The tables had turned and the conflict had taken an unexpected twist. Dechen, overwhelmed by the facts, ended up exploding. "This is outrageous!" he yelled. "It's a conspiracy planned between Tenzin and Lobsang to discredit my good name. The accusation doesn't have a leg to stand on. It's my word against the word of a boy and a woman. I won't tolerate it!"

Lobsang immediately put a stop to all the nonsense Dechen was blurting out in his anger and desperation, even though every statement that left his mouth, far from fixing things, represented one more nail in his coffin. It was time to put an end to this business once and for all. "Dechen, you've committed a crime in the parajika category, and I would go so far as to say, without any risk of being mistaken, that you've done it repeatedly. Therefore, you must leave the community."

A deep silence followed Lobsang's sentence. Very few of those present had ever witnessed an expulsion, not to mention one in such unheard-of circumstances.

Dechen folded his arms and looked at Lobsang, flatly challenging his verdict. He was not prepared to budge.

Lobsang shook his head. It was clear that the old lama was ready to fight to the last moment. And the irony of it all was that he could not force him to obey his decision. The legal system of Theravada monastic Buddhism laid down that the community could not judge a monk who refused to acknowledge his faults. Ultimately, it came down to a question of honesty and respect between the monk and the disciplinary code.

The situation seemed to have reached a dead end. What should Lobsang do next? Go on with the ceremony and deal with the matter of the expulsion at the end? Wouldn't that mean that Dechen would be getting his own way in the presence of the whole community? Lobsang was thinking fast, but no matter how much he thought about it he could see no way out. It was Dorjee, whose participation as master of ceremonies seemed to have been forgotten, who took the first step toward resolving the situation.

The young lama stood in front of Dechen and, without even bothering to part his lips, turned on his feet, with his back to the old lama.

The disconcerted look on Dechen's face was obvious. What was this nonsense? At first the rest of the audience did not seem to understand the gesture, but Tenzin immediately interpreted Dorjee's intention as if she had read his mind. The abbess imitated him and so did all the bhikkhuni. The entire block of Buddhist nuns turned their backs on Dechen in perfect harmony, like a squadron performing a maneuver. Then the others began to glimpse the picture to which Dorjee, amazingly inspired, had applied the first brushstroke. They were giving Lama Dechen nothing less than the *patta nikujjana kamma*, the punishment reserved to the lay faithful who seriously deviated from the teachings of the Buddha.

"What are you doing?" howled Dechen. "This is ridiculous!"

Many of the other monks, also seeing the measure as fitting, followed the example of Dorjee and the bhikkhuni in an unstoppable wave, in spite of Dechen's protests. More than a few of the monks had had enough of the old lama's extreme attitudes and erratic behavior. The novices also turned around, tired of the contempt he was in the habit of showing them. Even his own disciples, who had held out for so long under the pressure of a noble sense of loyalty, ended up joining the improvised rebellion. Dechen was beside himself, shouting furiously and waving his arms as he realized helplessly how he was becoming more and more isolated.

"Stop! That's enough, I'm telling you!" In his fury Dechen grabbed at some of the monks, trying in vain to make them turn round. "You can't do this to me! It's against the rules!"

It was true, they could not, but they had, and now no matter where he looked he only saw backs which expressed a unanimous, all-encompassing rejection. Although Dechen was surrounded at that moment by more than three hundred people, never in his whole life had he felt so alone.

Cornered, Dechen started to collapse. His shouts and theatrical gestures stopped. It had been a hard struggle, but it seemed that at last he was beginning to accept his defeat. And more than that, his guilt.

When he raised his gaze, he saw that only one person had not turned his back on him. Lobsang approached the old man slowly, put a hand on his shoulder, and looked him in the eye. Dechen seemed a different person, having shed the armor he had used to deceive himself and the Buddhist principles he had come to love so much. But it was too late for laments or apologies.

Dechen lowered his head and accepted his fate. However, he headed toward the exit without admitting to Lobsang that he had indeed committed the parajika crime which had brought about his expulsion, even though acceptance of the punishment was in itself sufficient admission of guilt.

For several days they didn't talk about anything else at the Batang Monastery. Events of that caliber did not occur every day. Some boasted that they had seen Dechen's spiritual decline coming for years, but few imagined he could have deviated so far from the path of purity. This was a serious warning to the entire body of monks, for if one lama had allowed himself to be carried away by human passions to such an extent, it could happen to anybody who failed to strive sufficiently hard. In the end Lobsang, as he had intended, had solved the problem which had obliged him to stay in Batang during the spring, even though he deeply regretted that the solution had been reached in such a cruel way.

But Dechen was already part of the past, and now Lobsang devoted much of his energy to young Thupten. After all, the abbot had found his new role as tutor fascinating and, as with everything he did, was working hard to obtain the best results. His present task consisted in trying to find out, as was the usual procedure with any new novice who entered the monastery, whether Thupten possessed any above average natural talent or ability, and if so, to guide him in that direction.

There was an enormous range of specialties, intellectual as well as artistic. And if he did not excel in any of them, as sometimes happened, he could always devote himself to more mundane but no less important tasks like cleaning or the maintenance of the monastic precinct.

To Lobsang's disappointment, after a week of submitting Thupten to different tests, it did not seem as if his disciple possessed any special quality.

First he spoke with the monks who taught in the school for novices. When he asked them whether Thupten showed any gift for studying, in which case he could have begun a course which would lead to the grade of lama, as Dorjee had done in his day, they said that, on the contrary, the boy did not seem to have an especially brilliant mind.

"Perhaps he shows a gift for meditation?" Lobsang asked. If that were so, in future he could receive special training in retreats far from the monastery where Thupten himself could find out whether or not he had a vocation for asceticism, as was sometimes the case.

"Are you serious?" they told him. "This boy is too energetic; with luck we manage to make him concentrate on one thing for more than a minute on end!"

Maybe Thupten could find his destiny, thought Lobsang, in the pictorial arts, which were highly developed in the Tibetan monastic tradition. So one afternoon he left him with the painter monks, to let them give him a chance and test his talent. At the time the artists were working on a *tanka*, a painting on cotton cloth which could be rolled up later and transported anywhere. They gave Thupten his own small canvas, as well as natural pigments for drawing and applying color.

"He's had a great time," they told Lobsang afterward. "There's no doubt of that. But honestly, we don't sense any great gift as an artist there."

Perhaps, thought Lobsang, his skittish disciple might be a success as a craftsman. A group of monks used clay with great skill to make statues and other decorative ornaments. This material in particular adapted well to the climate of the high plateau, to the point that the pieces did not even need to be fired, as the purity and dryness of the air were enough to preserve them well. Unfortunately, Thupten did not show much skill in the art of sculpture either.

Music was Lobsang's last resort, so that same evening the *umze*, as the person responsible for that discipline was called, took charge of Thupten to find out his ability with the various instruments and give him a singing test.

When Lobsang returned Thupten waved at him and went on banging a drum, a broad smile on his face. The umze moved a few steps away to inform Lobsang of the results, although seeing the expression on his face the abbot prepared for the worst once again.

"Does he have a good voice?" Lobsang asked without much conviction.

"Don't be offended, Lobsang," the umze said without beating around the bush, "but if you want me to be honest, there are goats in the fields who are more in tune than our good Thupten. And of course the boy is charming. Although I have to say he's been banging that drum for more than half an hour, and I'm getting a little tired of it."

"Even I am starting to get a headache," Lobsang admitted.

"His musical instinct is totally absent," the umze went on, "He's tried the kangling, the horn, the drum, and the cymbals. Although he puts a lot into it, he can't keep the rhythm or get a decent sound out of any of those instruments."

"Perhaps in the future…?"

The umze did not even reply; he merely shrugged. But quite apart from all that, whether he was more or less talented or more or less intelligent, it was his other qualities, such as his compassion and honesty, which made Lobsang tremendously proud of his pupil.

Just then Thupten came up to them holding something in his hands that had arrested his attention.

"I haven't tried this instrument," he said. "May I?"

"It's a conch," said the umze. "It's the most complicated of all instruments to get a sound out of, because you need to master the technique of continuous breathing, which allows you to play and breathe at the same time so that you can perform long pieces without any interruption." After this explanation, he sent him off with his permission to try it. After all, it would not hurt. "It took me years to learn to play the conch," he told Lobsang. "It takes a lot of practice, although few instruments are so gratifying once you master them."

He had not finished the sentence when a sweet, harmonious melody drifted to the ears of both lamas in an almost mysterious way. The umze and the abbot turned round to see before them a picture that could not possibly be real. And yet it was. Thupten was playing the conch with a skill that the most expert musicians themselves would have longed for.

The umze's jaw dropped several inches. "I've never seen such a prodigy in my whole life," was all he could manage to mutter.

Nor had Lobsang, but for him it was only one more reason to feel proud of Thupten.

* * *

Summer slipped in through the mountains without any noise, and the habitually sharp air that swept the outside of the cave each morning was transformed into a warm breeze. An explosion of reds bathed the valleys and rocky masses, while the water of the swollen rivers took on a sheen of emerald green. Only the highest peaks continued to show their perennial white image on the horizon.

Life in the mountains had turned into a routine for Chögyam. Of course they led a contemplative life, but at the same time it demanded a great effort, given that it was reduced to mere meditation and the repetition of the same mantras and prayers ad infinitum. And surely no other boy but Chögyam, thanks to his own self-possessed nature, would have been able to bear it. Luckily his master's teachings alleviated the tedium and roused Chögyam's interest in the way of dharma. Also, from time to time he enjoyed his moments of leisure, for which the hermit had given him another wooden figure representing an ancient Tibetan warrior. However, Chögyam did not understand the great mental discipline the hermit lama subjected him to so insistently.

"My duty is to prepare you for a crucial moment," he would say in reply to each question.

And little else did he manage to find out, although Chögyam suspected this was because not even the hermit himself knew the details.

But as the summer season drew on, Chögyam noticed that there were changes in the routines which were unfamiliar. The hermit had begun to spend less time teaching him and had also stopped carving. By contrast, he had significantly lengthened his long sessions of meditation, in the course of which he sank into ever deeper lethargies.

This strange attitude followed a prompting which the hermit felt was transcendental, and which for the time being he had not wanted to share with his disciple. And this was that the spark of life within the old man was flickering, beginning to fail and already foretelling its disappearance. The hermit had become aware of his coming departure and was preparing himself for death.

At last the day came. Chögyam woke up one morning and immediately noticed the hermit's failing state. The lama remained seated in the meditation posture but was obliged to lean his back against the wall of the cave. His breathing was barely audible, and his eyes had unmistakably lost any trace of color.

Chögyam bent over him, his face frozen with worry. "Master, do you feel all right?"

"It's my time, Chögyam." His voice was no more than a thread of air, devoid of substance.

"It can't be," he begged vainly. Then he took his hand, a wrinkled claw with long twisted nails, cold as ice. Chögyam's eyes moistened, and for a few seconds, through the veil of tears that had formed on his retinas, he saw with fascination that the hermit was indeed wearing a black hat on his head, just as he had once told him. The vision of the hat, which looked to him more like a crown, vanished at the first blink, but not the words of his master telling him that if he were ever to see it, he would then become its wearer. "Master, what will I do without your help?"

"You have a shelter, and you also know where to find food and water. Keep meditating and don't forget what I've taught you."

"But during the winter conditions are very different. I won't even be able to bear the cold."

"Don't you worry," the hermit said. "Before winter arrives, they'll have found you."

Chögyam struggled to hold back his tears. A knot had formed in his stomach, and the cave had never seemed as small to him as it did at that moment.

"Pay attention to me, Chögyam. I'll now enter *tukdam*, the last meditation. It's a state of deep abstraction that will serve as a bridge on the way to my death," the hermit explained. "Well, if during this process I get to the highest level of spiritual realization and I reach Awakening, my material body will be absorbed by the essence of its constituent elements and be transformed into light, leaving behind only my nails and hair."

Chögyam nodded, trying to take in his master's words.

"This prodigy, well-known among yogis and Tibetan Buddhist sages, is known as the "rainbow body" because it's accompanied by the spontaneous appearance of lights in the sky." The hermit lama had to pause for air before going on. Chögyam was listening with great attention. "You'll wait three days, from tomorrow. On the fourth you'll check the state of my body. If it's still present, you must drag it to the shelf on the north side of the mountain, to our usual place of meditation, and leave it there until the angels of the heavens, the dakini, have taken it away. Do you understand?"

"Yes, master, perfectly well," Chögyam said. "But I was thinking... what if we save ourselves all this difficult business and you postpone your death until some other time, as far in the future as possible?"

The hermit gave a wry smile, but shook his head. "I'm afraid that's not in my power," he said.

Chögyam resigned himself and squeezed his master's hand in a sincere attempt to show him his affection.

Shortly afterward the hermit took his leave with the last breath of his voice and closed his eyes to begin a journey from which he would never return.

Chögyam intended to cling to his daily routine for the rest of the day, but in the event he kept the hermit company for almost the whole time, even though the old man was not even moving and his breathing was reduced to a minimum. It was a day he would always remember blurrily, as if a thick mist had clouded his mind to protect him from the memory.

Next morning Chögyam found that the hermit had stopped breathing and showed no signs of life. Then he began to count the three days he had promised to wait to see what happened to the old man's body. Chögyam had more than enough time to weep for his master, and afterward to feel intense fear in the face of the solitude that awaited him for an indefinite time.

On the morning of the second day Chögyam noticed a curious change in the hermit's body: he could have sworn it had shrunk slightly. The following day, his doubts were dispelled, as the shrinkage was immediately evident. The surprises followed one after another. Even more noticeable was that the body not only did not decay but gave off a pleasant smell.

Chögyam shared one more night with the hermit's corpse, and on the morning of the fourth day he was able to see the product of that wait. The body had not vanished, but had shrunk about eighteen inches to reach the size of a seven- or eight-year-old boy. What had happened was good proof of the high level of spiritual realization the lama hermit had reached, even though the "rainbow body" had not become apparent.

So it was time to move the body to the place the old man had pointed out to him, to fulfill his last will. Chögyam grasped it by the feet and pulled it along the perimeter of the mountain. The weight was no problem, as a sack of feathers would have been heavier. The hardest thing was feeling the hermit's skin tear to ribbons as he dragged the body up the rough terrain with its scattering of sharp pebbles and stones.

When he reached the ledge of rock which jutted out over the void, Chögyam walked along it and left the body on the edge of the abyss. Far behind him were the days when he was overcome by cold sweat and vertigo made his knees knock. He looked up. The sun shone with authority from its pinnacle in the sky. Chögyam moved away from the body and retreated to a point about ten yards away. He sat and waited to see what would happen.

It was not long before the first vulture appeared, quickly attracting all the rest. Shoving and flapping, an enormous flock congregated around the hermit's body to share in the unexpected feast. The carrion birds used their curved beaks to tear the skin and tendons, as well as extracting the marrow from the bones. Some of the vultures looked sideways at Chögyam, others more directly, but the boy held their gaze and none of them made any attempt to come closer.

The vultures made short work of the mortal remains of the hermit, feasting so eagerly that they left not a trace. Chögyam watched the angels take flight again and lose themselves in the distance. Then a giant rainbow appeared on the horizon, showing its palette of colors in perfect symmetry. And when the angels crossed it in their flight, Chögyam wondered whether the lama hermit had reached Awakening after all and entered Nirvana through the main gate, as he had always dreamed.

Once the celestial burial was over, Chögyam went back to the cave and prepared himself for his solitary life. Autumn was just around the corner.

* * *

Time was relentless, and the dates followed one another in the calendar without the appearance of any news worth mentioning at the Tsurphu Monastery.

With the boy from Shigatse they had used their last resort, and since that echoing failure there had not been the slightest indication to set them on the trail of a new candidate. So many mistakes had accumulated that not even the astrologers dared to make calculations or predictions, nor did the gurus and great lamas darc show off their gifts of clairvoyance.

The situation could not have been tenser, since apart from the frustration felt by those responsible for the Kagyu School at their own inability to find the tulku, there was the added pressure of the Emperor Kublai Khan's stated intention of meeting the Karmapa as an indispensable prerequisite for his conversion to Buddhism. At least they were not expecting the Emperor for a year, given that his ruling commitments prevented him from traveling to Tibet, and the Mongol representative they had been told would be sent with the mission to supervise them had not arrived either.

All the same, Kyentse was upset, because during the previous week he had been having the same dream over and over again. A dream in which his old master, the late Karmapa, was trying to communicate with him and give him some information. Kyentse had no doubt that it was the sign they had long been waiting for, and that his dream held the key which would put them on the trail of the real tulku, even though so far he had not been able to disentangle any meaning that might lead to practical results.

Yet Kyentse did not despair, and after realizing that he would not get any clear ideas by himself, he decided to share his dream with Tsultrim and hear his opinion.

The abbot was flattered by this and gave full attention to Kyentse's account. In his dream, the monk appeared in the midst of a blinding light which bathed everything around him. Kyentse then began to walk, until a few steps further on he heard the echo of the word "Karmapa," reverberating and amplified, as if the sound came from a mountain echo. The voice was unfamiliar, so Kyentse went on through the brightness, noticing that the outline of the light decreased gradually with every step he took until the situation turned upside down and ended by swallowing up his own frame of reference in absolute darkness. In the new scene the voice stopped, and after a brief silence was clearly replaced by that of his dear master, who was reciting his favorite mantra over and over again: *Om mane padme hum.*

"And after that?" Tsultrim asked.

"Nothing. That's all I can remember."

The abbot scratched his skull and pondered, while Kyentse gazed at him attentively.

"There's no doubt that the dream holds a meaning we're unable to grasp at first sight," said the abbot.

"I concur exactly."

The abbot racked his brains to find some less conventional way of interpreting the dream.

"I'm intrigued by the metamorphosis of light into darkness." Tsultrim was thinking at top speed, putting the ideas that came to his mind straight into words. "And from a more prosaic point of view, I find it striking that the Karmapa died reciting the mantra of your dream."

Kyentse pondered about the abbot's words, letting them settle inside him. Then he felt a spark in his heart such as he had not experienced for a long time. This was his inspiration, which under the spur of Tsultrim's observations had finally taken shape. "That's it!" he exclaimed, seizing Tsultrim by the shoulders and shaking him gently. "The key is in what you just said."

"Can you explain that?"

"The Karmapa never stopped reciting that mantra on his deathbed; we both agree on that. But don't you remember that apart from that, just before he gave up his last breath, he grasped the *ghau* that lay on his chest?"

"Yes, that's right."

"Tsultrim, are you aware of whether anybody examined its contents?"

The abbot slapped his forehead, realizing the terrible mistake they had made from the beginning. At the time they had carried out a routine search among the belongings of the Karmapa so as to find out whether he had left a letter indicating the whereabouts of the tulku, a practice for which there was more than one precedent. But Tsultrim was sure that nobody had inspected the ghau, as it was not usual to open the protective amulets of those who had died.

Tsultrim shook his head. "If I didn't do it and neither did you, I doubt whether any other monk would have done it."

"Let's find out, then!" urged Kyentse.

Both lamas, unable to contain themselves, raced down the halls of the monastery before the astonished eyes of their fellow lamas, who had never seen the abbot and the Rinpoche so flustered, in such a hurry, and holding up the skirts of their robes to move faster.

As soon as they reached the private rooms of the Karmapa, where his belongings were kept intact, they regained their breath and lost no time in finding the pendant.

Kyentse held the ghau in his hands, while Tsultrim watched anxiously. They were expecting that the tiny box of prayers stuck to the metal would contain a piece of paper folded several times, on which, in addition to the Karmapa's favorite mantra, there would be some words in his own writing alluding to the whereabouts of the tulku.

"Open it at once!" urged Tsultrim.

Kyentse lifted the cover, and a piece of parchment slipped through his fingers. His hands were shaking uncontrollably. He unfolded it. On one side was the well-known mantra, and on the reverse a message left by the Karmapa before he died, in which he indicated the circumstances of his rebirth.

The two monks looked at each other as if they were unable to believe the discovery after seven years of fruitless search. Then a great happiness overcame them, and they clasped one another in an affectionate embrace.

They read the letter so many times that they soon knew it by heart. The writing of the Karmapa read as follows:

In Tibetan lands, to the east of here.
In the region of the celestial rivers.
Opening up the landscape, the Lotus Valley.
My sanctuary, a shadowy cavity.
Over me sweet tears pour.
And under me, a legion of pillars.

The content of the message was as cryptic as might have been expected, but the ambiguity, the imprecision, and the double meaning of the words were the norm in that very singular type of writing. Now it was their turn to scrutinize every sentence, interpret the literal meaning of the words and also read between the lines.

The first two verses clearly specified the Kham region. This was located in Eastern Tibet, and some of the most important rivers of Asia ran through its lands. There was no doubt about that point, and all those they consulted on the subject agreed. However, Kham covered a vast stretch of land, so it seemed crucial to narrow down the search area. The answer had to be in the third verse, but here they had come up against a problem which had them baffled, for after consulting the wisest sages, all had agreed that nowhere in all Kham—and indeed all Tibet—was a valley of that name. And as far as the remaining verses were concerned, everyone agreed that they would make no sense until the previous one had been clarified.

Nevertheless, the experts admitted the possibility that there might be some tiny nameless valley which the locals might refer to by the name in the letter. All in all, finding it was not going to be an easy task.

"We should go to Kham and find out on the land for ourselves," suggested Kyentse.

"Out of the question," replied Tsultrim. "We don't know the area, and we'd end up getting in the way of our own interests. We should ask someone we trust and who is familiar with the region."

Kyentse's face lit up after only a few moments. "I have the very man!" he declared. "Lama Lobsang Geshe, a dear old colleague."

The abbot hardly needed a second to consider the proposal. "Of course!" he said. "His training is excellent, not to mention his determination and meticulousness. How long is it since he left Tsurphu?"

"Ten years. The length of time he's been in charge of the Batang Monastery. Although I know he spends most of his time on the roads, preaching the teachings of the Buddha around all the villages and hamlets he finds on his way. If he doesn't know the Lotus Valley, I've no doubt he'll find it."

"That's that, then," Tsultrim concluded. "Shall we send him a letter with the details of the mission?"

"No, we'll ask him to come," Kyentse decided. "The importance of the quest deserves to be explained in person. Besides, I'd like him to read the Karmapa's original letter for himself, to touch the ghau, and to walk through his rooms until he's fully immersed in his energy and his memory."

The decision was made. That same day, a messenger left for Batang with an urgent errand for Lama Lobsang Geshe.

CHAPTER V

Fall

"Even a novice who dedicates himself to the doctrine of the sublime awakening illuminates this world like a moon emerging from the clouds."

Dhammapada, 382

At the Batang Monastery everything went on according to the routine. Thupten had grown used to his life as a novice, and Lobsang was planning to renew his missionary activities throughout the wide region of Kham.

But the situation took an unexpected turn with the arrival of a messenger from Gurum, who brought a letter signed by the lamas responsible for the Tsurphu Gompa. The letter urged Lobsang to go back as soon as he could to the place where he had received his training as a Buddhist monk. It did not explain the reason, but it might be guessed to be a truly exceptional one. Lobsang could not imagine what it might be about, nor could he guess why his attendance was so important. All the same, he would acquiesce and put himself at the disposal of the leaders of the Kagyu School.

Lobsang finished his preparations for the journey, which he would make with a couple of monks from Batang and a nomad caravan they would share the journey with along most of the route. Thupten was to join the expedition too. For the young boy, Lobsang's presence was still essential, so he insisted on going with him and promised repeatedly not to cause trouble. Lobsang made no objection. The trip was in no way an obstacle to his work as tutor, and in fact he would take advantage of it to continue with his pupil's training and study certain subjects in more depth. However, Thupten was obliged to leave behind the precious conch—which he played as often as he could—as the monastery had only the one and it was needed for the offices and ceremonies.

During the first stretch of the journey, when they crossed the mountain pass toward the west, Thupten immediately recognized the place which had witnessed his family's tragedy. Lobsang noticed that the boy trembled and several tears welled up in his eyes, on the verge of rolling down his cheeks. Thupten's grimace once again brought to mind that of the sad, defenseless boy he had found on a street of Batang.

"Don't look at the cliff," he urged as he held him in a comforting hug. "You'd better close your eyes. We'll soon leave this place behind."

"I was falling and my brother was already safe, you know? But at the last moment a gust of wind changed everything. It really should have been me, not Chögyam, the one to fall to the bottom of that valley."

The journey turned out to be quite tiring, but as he had promised, Thupten did not complain even once. The roads were quite busy during that time of year. On their way they met robust merchants who carried their wares in wooden frames on their backs and large nomad families who were moving to less inhospitable lands with their herds of animals, in search of a place to spend the winter. Occasional showers made them stop and seek temporary cover from their fury as they made their way down slippery slopes. The next minute they would enjoy a glorious view of the Tibetan plain, as flat and bright as the roof of any Buddhist temple.

Three weeks later they sighted Gurum in the distance, and very soon afterward the magnificent Tsurphu Gompa, surrounded by a colorful spider's web of innumerable prayer banners. Thupten could not believe what he saw, as if his eyes were set upon showing him a reality that could not possibly be true. The impressive monastic city, with its own streets and buildings, triumphed in comparison to the Batang Monastery, since it was at least four times its size. The main access consisted of a transit zone through which hundreds of monks went in and out, each on his own mission and duty, meticulously assigned. Although overwhelmed, Thupten felt comfortable there at once.

Lobsang had last visited Tsurphu for the Karmapa's funeral, and that was seven years ago now. The place inspired in him a profound feeling of longing and of course fondness. After all, he had spent most of his life behind those walls, since his family, realizing the impossibility of feeding him, had given him to the Buddhist monks when he was a child not much older than Thupten. The gompa had not changed at all since he had left a decade before, and Lobsang had no doubt that whatever might happen, he would always be able to see that little corner of Tibet as a second home, where perhaps he would return in the future, to savor his old age as he had his childhood and youth.

Lobsang announced his arrival, and in only a couple of minutes his old friend Kyentse Rinpoche came out to welcome him, with a smile which clearly expressed the joy he felt at seeing him there at last. Both lamas bowed with their palms together in the customary greeting and hugged each other with the love grown out of sharing many years of studies and experiences. Although life had taken them down different paths, the strong bond between them would never be broken.

Surprisingly, Thupten, perhaps imitating his master, also threw himself enthusiastically at Kyentse, who could barely lift him up and hold him in his arms, as at his age the boy was quite heavy.

"I didn't know you were so good with children," teased Lobsang.

"Neither did I, at least until now," replied Kyentse, putting the boy down. "Did you have a good trip?"

"Wearisome, as they all are. But what matters is that we're here at last."

Kyentse nodded, pleased. "Lobsang, forgive the hurry, but the matter for which we asked you to visit can't wait. You must come with me right away to see the abbot, so we can explain the reason why we wrote to you."

"Of course."

"Meanwhile, the monks and the novice who accompany you are free to walk around the gompa at liberty."

Lobsang realized at once that Kyentse was leading him to the late Karmapa's rooms, which surprised him, since tradition ordered that nothing should be altered until his successor had been found.

"What's the matter? Have you found the tulku?"

"Not yet," said Kyentse. "That's the problem, precisely."

They reached their destination, where Tsultrim Trungpa was waiting anxiously, as was usual with him. Some of the tension in the abbot of Tsurphu's face faded when he saw Lobsang appear at the door, followed by Kyentse. "I'm grateful to you for agreeing to our request so promptly," he said.

"I'm at your disposal," Lobsang replied.

Tsultrim went straight to the point and explained in detail the process which had brought them to their present position. From the beginning, the search for the tulku had been an unprecedented failure. The candidates came one after another, but none managed to pass even the preliminary test. The astrologers had not been accurate in their predictions, and neither had the committee of wise monks been able to use their famous gift of clairvoyance. Until at last, very recently, and through a repeated dream of Kyentse's, they had found a note left by the Karmapa himself in which he identified the clues for locating his future reincarnation.

"The Karmapa had hidden the note inside his ghau," said Kyentse. "That's why we overlooked it at first."

"Perhaps the Karmapa's wish was that you wouldn't find it before time," Lobsang said. "And only when the right moment came, he let you know through the recurring dream you had."

Tsultrim and Kyentse exchanged glances. They had also toyed with that possibility, which sounded even more plausible when Lobsang mentioned it.

"But... what's my role in all this?" Lobsang asked.

Tsultrim merely handed him the small piece of parchment that contained the message left by the Karmapa.

Lobsang read it in silence, without any change in his expression. "I see..." he murmured. "It's evident that the tulku is within the region of Kham, although I'm sorry to say that I've never heard of the Lotus Valley."

Tsultrim and Kyentse could not hide their disappointment, even though they were not really surprised.

"Anyhow," said Kyentse, "we're convinced that you're the right person to carry out this mission."

Lobsang considered the proposition for a few moments. "It's a great responsibility, as is the trust you honor me with," he said. "If this valley exists, I can assure you I'll find it, and I'll locate the tulku as well."

Lobsang read the note again, looked at the Karmapa's ghau, and then examined the rest of his personal effects. Tsultrim and Kyentse left him to it in silence until Lobsang seemed satisfied. Then they gave him some more information that might be of use to him, regarding the omens which surrounded the death of the Karmapa and his last words on his deathbed. Lobsang seemed to absorb all this information with the same ease he had always showed in studying and which had allowed him to reach the level of Geshe at such a young age.

"But there's more," Tsultrim said. "Another matter, directly related, that we need to tell you about."

Lobsang frowned. He had the feeling he was not going to like this other part at all.

"Drogön Chögyal Phagpa, the leader of the Sakya School, is at Kublai Khan's court introducing him to the teachings of the Buddha, in which the emperor has shown a more than significant interest. So it's more than likely that Kublai Khan is going to convert to Buddhism." Tsultrim paused dramatically before going on. "But the Mongol emperor won't make a final decision without first meeting the Karmapa…"

"Something that is currently impossible," Lobsang pointed out.

"Exactly," Tsultrim confirmed. "What's more, the emperor doesn't trust the process of succession, so he's sent a Mongol representative to guarantee that we don't bypass the established rules."

"That's ridiculous," said Lobsang. "We, more than anyone else, have an interest in making no mistake in the choice of the tulku, and we'd definitely never manipulate his naming according to spurious interests or of any other kind."

"That goes without saying, but the one who gives the orders is the emperor," said Tsultrim. "And we have no alternative. The Mongol representative will go with you in your search and will make sure there's no fraud and that everything gets done in an exemplary manner."

After this revelation Lobsang became aware that the weight of his responsibility had doubled, and the pressure he was already feeling was immediately multiplied by two. Despite this, he did not shrink in the slightest and accepted with determination the significant task they had placed in his hands.

Then they showed Lobsang to the rooms allocated to illustrious visitors, where the Mongol representative was already installed. His name was Kunnu, and he had been welcomed with all due honors.

"He's an extremely reserved man," Kyentse explained. "He never leaves the precinct, and the monks try to avoid him at all costs."

When he found himself in the presence of the Mongol, Lobsang was struck by the contrast between his good manners and the roughness of his looks. Kunnu was short and bordering on fifty, but he had kept a powerful physique, so that very few would have dared to confront him. His clothing consisted of a fur hat with ear flaps, cassock, and heavy leather boots. Lobsang would have sworn it was a military uniform, particularly the most striking element which finished off the picture: a double curved saber, which more than anything else made Lobsang, from the start, distrust the mysterious envoy from the Imperial Court.

He and Kunnu measured each other with a glance for a few eternal seconds. They did not know each other and they belonged to totally different cultures, but it did not escape either that from that moment on they would be spending a great deal of time together on the trail of the tulku.

"We're leaving tomorrow," Lobsang said.

Considering the forced company he would have to drag along with him permanently, as personified by the enigmatic Mongol, Lobsang did not think it wise to take Thupten with him. He decided it would be best to leave him at the Tsurphu Monastery, where he would have everything he needed and would be well taken care of, then pick him up again when they finally came back from their uncertain mission. The problem lay in how Thupten would take the news; up till then he had never been away from his side, ever since his rescue in the streets of Batang.

Inevitably he found his pupil in the musical instrument room, where he was asking the umze for permission to play the conch. Lobsang explained his plans, using the utmost tact over each word so that Thupten would understand his decision and not think for a moment that he was abandoning him. To Lobsang's surprise Thupten did not seem to mind the news at all, and his only condition was that the lama who had welcomed them at the door should be his tutor during Lobsang's absence.

Kyentse didn't hesitate to accept the request which Lobsang expressed in terms of a personal favor. He promised not only to care for the wellbeing of the boy but also to continue with his education from the point where they had left off. Thupten was also assured that he would be able to play the conch any time he wanted to, since in Tsurphu there were plenty for all the music apprentices. Besides, his extraordinary talent was sure to inspire the other novices.

On the morning of their departure the temperature dropped significantly. The sun was no more than a timid golden blur, hidden by a cluster of black clouds whose brightness barely reached the stupas arranged on the four cardinal points of the monastery. Thupten put his arms around Lobsang's waist and pressed his face against his stomach.

"Be good and always do what Kyentse tells you," Lobsang told him as he returned the heartfelt hug.

Thupten nodded. He could not speak due to the knot he felt in his throat. He was happy in Tsurphu but also saddened by his master's departure.

Without further ado, Lobsang turned toward the exit, where Kunnu was waiting for him mounted on a wild Mongol horse. His hieratic face showed no feeling at all, whether of friendliness or aversion.

* * *

On the way to Batang, the Mongol representative tried at all costs to keep his distance from the Buddhist monks.

Lobsang led the way together with the two monks who were accompanying him, while Kunnu brought up the rear several yards behind, establishing a barrier of silence between the two sides which only splintered when they had to decide practical questions about the vicissitudes of the journey. Nevertheless, Lobsang was determined to resist this rule of silence imposed by the Mongol. He tried by all means to get close to him and engage him in conversation so that he could get to know him better, with the aim of creating a minimum of trust which seemed to him as shocking as it was necessary.

Kunnu turned out to be a genuinely tough nut to crack, and Lobsang had to work hard to drag the odd word out of him which might shed a little light on his past. Despite this, in the end he managed to find out that the Mongol was a retired general who now served the Great Khan in diplomatic and other missions. Therefore, his worst suspicions were sadly confirmed. Lobsang was now side by side with someone who had made violence his trade and had devoted much of his life to annihilating other human beings in unfair wars perpetrated under the auspices of the powerful. So, he was at the opposite extreme of the pacifist philosophy preached by the Buddhist monks, by virtue of which the gift of life was the most precious good, beyond any differences of race, religion, or flag.

Lobsang took advantage of the long journey to plan his course of action. He would begin his inquiries in Batang, and if he did not get any results he would head east, stopping in every province until he had swept every inch of the Kham region. The search would take months, of that he was perfectly sure, since quite apart from the enormous area of land he would have to cover, he had decided to follow up any lead, no matter how small or insignificant. Lobsang was fully aware that he would be dependent on the inhabitants of each province for details of the mysterious valley he was looking for, which did not appear on any map of Tibet. Many would be obliged to leave their chores in order to help him find it, with all the disruption that would entail. Thus, with the aim of stimulating their cooperation and also to help finance their journey, the lamas at Tsurphu had provided him with a splendid sum of money which Kunnu had taken upon him to guard with a zeal bordering on the obsessive.

As soon as they reached Batang, Lobsang told Dorjee, who had already been ordained as lama, all the details of the mission he had been entrusted with. Then he contacted the local authorities so that they could spread the news among the population that the Buddhist monks needed the help of nomads, merchants, peasants; in short, of everyone who regarded themselves as knowledgeable about the region, and that their collaboration would be generously rewarded.

The following day, drawn by the tempting reward, the flow of candidates did not stop all morning, surpassing Lobsang's expectations. To receive them they had prepared one of the halls of the monastery, in which Lobsang himself, with Dorjee on one side and Kunnu on the other, sat on the floor waiting, as if they were a tribunal, although instead of judging they only wanted to gather information. The difficulties of the task soon became evident when after spending a whole day interviewing locals, each one more knowledgeable than the one before, none of them were able to tell them anything about any valley which might be named after the Lotus or give them the slightest hint as to where it might lie.

Lobsang was prepared to listen to the volunteers who came to the monastery for two more days, but if in this time nobody provided them with a clue he would cross Batang off his list and move to the next province to continue his search, which had really just begun. Nevertheless, a candidate appeared in the evening whose intervention would turn out to be less fruitless than that of the rest.

The man before them avoided looking directly into their eyes; his appearance was dirty even though he tried to hide the fact, and he kept one of his hands hidden behind his back.

"He's an outlaw," Dorjee whispered in Lobsang's ear.

"I'll be brief," the abbot whispered back. "We have nothing to lose by questioning him."

Wangchuk remained standing there looking unfriendly, watching the lamas whispering to each other. Lobsang distrusted the fellow at once, but for lack of specific details he never associated him with the ruthless man who had hurt Thupten so much. "What's your name," he asked.

Wangchuk gave a false name. He hated having had to go there after swearing he would never step across the threshold's monastery again in his life, least of all taking into account the risk he ran if Thupten saw him there and finally decided to report him for the crimes he had committed against him. Nevertheless, his desperate situation, which had noticeably worsened since the boy's departure, had left him no alternative. The lure of money had been a more powerful temptation than his burning hatred toward the Buddhists or the fear of further punishment. All in all, if he had replied to the announcement it was because he really fit the profile, since during his years as a shepherd he had acquired a detailed knowledge of Batang and its borderlands.

"Do you know or have you ever heard of the Lotus Valley?"

"No," Wangchuk replied after searching his memory. "At least not here in Batang, I'm sure of that."

"It's what we feared," said Lobsang. "All the other candidates have said the same thing."

The feeling of disappointment filled both parties. The monks were beginning to be frustrated with the endless list of denials, while Wangchuk was cursing himself over the lost opportunity to earn a substantial amount of money.

"Although..." A forgotten memory crossed his mind.

Lobsang leaned forward and encouraged him to go on. The outlaw's gesture, as if something had come to his mind all of a sudden, seemed genuine and not merely a trick to catch their attention.

"I know of a very narrow valley which doesn't even have a name. On the side of the mountain you can make out something odd sticking out, and if you see it from the right perspective, it looks like the outline of a lotus flower carved into the mountain rock."

Wangchuk, who did not have much imagination, had made out that shape in the rock many years ago, encouraged by the influence of alcohol—a fact he preferred to omit to avoid making his story sound less credible.

Lobsang nodded. Of course it was not much of a lead, but it was worth following through to see how far it took them. It was also the only one he had been able to gather all day.

"Could you guide us to this place?" he asked.

Wangchuk congratulated himself on realizing he had aroused the lama's interest. He had not thought he would be taken seriously, not to mention that he would have created such expectations.

"And... could you tell me how much money the reward is?"

Dorjee and Lobsang looked at each other and exchanged impressions in a low voice.

"I don't trust him," Dorjee insisted.

"I don't like him either, but I'm convinced he's telling the truth."

The Mongol general took out a handful of coins from the leather bag that rested on his thighs. Wangchuk's eyes sparkled at the brightness of the metal.

"We'll give you half if you take us to the place you've described and the other half if we find what we're looking for there," Kunnu said in his first intervention during the whole interview.

The amount the Mongol was holding in his hand already seemed attractive to Wangchuk, but to imagine the whole sum in that pouch, perhaps twenty times more, nearly left him breathless.

"But I'm warning you, if what you've told us about this strange formation in the rock isn't true," Lobsang said, "then you'll leave empty-handed."

"It's a deal," the outlaw said.

"Good. It will be getting dark soon. We'll leave tomorrow morning."

Wangchuk led them to the mountain pass which preceded the access to Batang. Only Kunnu and Lobsang had gone with the outlaw, since Dorjee had remained at the monastery to interview the volunteers who would be coming that day. The three men moved on foot, as Wangchuk had assured them that the spot was very near. However, after half an hour walking along the path on the edge of the cliff, battered by the early freezing breeze from the snow-capped peaks, the trek soon became harder than they had expected.

Lobsang looked around and recognized the approximate spot where Thupten had told him, amid sobs, that he had lost his family because of a terrible storm.

"It was around here," muttered Wangchuk to himself, as he looked at the mountain on the other side of the abyss, which rose from the foot of a cedar wood buried in the bowl of the narrow valley.

Lobsang was beginning to doubt the usefulness of this excursion as he observed the constant signs of uncertainty on the part of the outlaw, who if anything seemed to be going on blindly. Wangchuk could read the distrust in the lama's eyes, which did not help him at all except to make him more nervous and pressure him more than was necessary. The only one who remained impassive was Kunnu, who, while paying close attention to everything around him, stayed put in his own bubble of silence.

"There! I can see it!" Wangchuk's enthusiastic shout echoed four times among the cliffs.

Lobsang discerned a hump standing out on the highest reach of the mountain side, not finding anything particular in that. He frowned and gave the outlaw a reproving look.

"You have to stand here and look at it from this angle," Wangchuk explained.

Lobsang complied reluctantly, more convinced every moment that the outlaw was making them waste precious time. Nothing could be further from the truth. From the right angle and in the right light, the play of edges and shadows created by the rock did indeed make it look like an immense lotus flower opening out of the mountain. Not until he had it before his eyes did Lobsang overcome his initial reservations and award this clue the importance it really deserved. "It's true…" he muttered.

"Indeed, as I said. And now can I have the first part of my reward?"

"Not until you guide us to the mountain," Lobsang replied. "And if we find what we're looking for there, you won't only receive half but all of it."

"But what is it you're looking for?"

Lobsang decided not to tell him the whole truth, but something that might serve the outlaw as a reference. "We're looking for a person," he said.

Wangchuk's face did not hide a clear grimace of incredulity. "A person? There? It's impossible. Why would anybody choose to go in there? The mountain is a lump of rock, very steep to ascend, and almost barren. Access to the valley from there is so complicated that in winter snow and ice block it completely. It's not even good for cattle grazing."

The Mongol representative did not think there could be anybody in the valley either, least of all a small child. Kunnu did not show what he was thinking, nor did he lose his composure, but he was sure they were chasing the shadows of a strange religion which he did not believe in, made up of shaven-headed contemplatives who subordinated the inheritance of their lineage to the belief in a miraculous reincarnation with little evidence based on fact.

"Once again, it's not possible," the outlaw insisted.

"You're probably right," Lobsang admitted. "But sometimes there are reasons that escape our intellect, usually those which have more to do with faith than reasoning. So… how do we get there?"

145

Wangchuk bit his tongue. Whether he liked it or not, the Buddhist was in charge; if he wanted his handful of coins he had no choice but to carry out his instructions. "All right," he said grudgingly.

Lobsang and Kunnu followed the outlaw along the mountain pass for half an hour more, along the path which left the range behind, and entered the high plateau dominated by grey plains. But before leaving the path that ran along the edge, Wangchuk made them stop and pointed to an abrupt hillock jutting out by the path at the spot where the cliff reached its lowest point.

Lobsang expressed his annoyance in the form of a long sigh.

Wangchuk shrugged. "It's the only point of access to the valley," he said.

"Well then, so be it."

The hill was extremely steep, and in some sections of their descent they had to use their hands to keep their balance and take support on the ground, which was covered with pebbles and treacherous scree. Wangchuk managed as best he could, somewhat more hampered than the others by the stump of his left arm.

Once down the hill, they turned into the wood of giant cedars. They still had a long stretch before reaching the side of the mountain which Lobsang had decided to explore, where high up was the curious outcrop that had led them there.

While he walked on, grumbling under his breath, Wangchuk came to realize what a marvelous opportunity fate had served him on a platter. Why limit himself to the reward he had been promised, which now did not seem so very much after all, if he could get away with everything the Mongol was carrying in his inseparable leather pouch? Until now murder had not figured in Wangchuk's record of crime, but... wasn't there a first time for everything? Of course the disappearance of those two individuals from the face of the earth would not cause any remorse to his conscience. Perhaps the exact opposite, as over time he would end up glorifying his feat. The Mongol was an invader, a foreigner who years before had spread terror throughout Tibet, so that his death might well be seen as an act of justice. As for the lama, he would be doing nothing more than consummating his longed-for revenge. The denunciation made by the abbot after his robbery in the temple had brought about the amputation of his left hand and the ruining of his life.

146

Little by little, as they went on, the idea gathered strength in the outlaw's imagination. His victims' bodies would never be found in the depths of this narrow valley, and if some day they were, he would already be far, far away. Maybe in Lhasa or Shigatse, any big city where he might go unnoticed and begin a new life with that handsome sum of money. He might start a business involving commerce, or perhaps cattle… anything which allowed him to say goodbye forever to his miserable existence. It was not a premeditated plan, but the circumstances were working so much in his favor that not to take advantage of the opportunity would be a folly he would regret for the rest of his life. The risk was high, of course, but so would be the reward if he were successful.

Wangchuk had to improvise a plan of action. He needed to find a vantage point in relation to his two targets, to catch them unawares and commit the crimes he had conceived. Without thinking twice, Wangchuk pretended to trip on a root and threw himself face down on the ground.

Lobsang bent over the outlaw, worried about the tremendous blow he had received. "Are you all right?"

Wangchuk grabbed one foot and clenched his teeth hard, to give the impression of being in intense pain. "It's not serious," he replied, "but we'll have to stop for a while. I can't walk right now."

"All right," Lobsang agreed. "We could all do with a bit of a rest."

Kunnu sat on a rock, already bored with an expedition he could see no sense in. Lobsang for his part sat down comfortably on the ground in the meditation posture. He had a feeling, a tingling in his stomach, that he was on the genuine trail of the tulku. It was hard to believe he could have been so lucky, but what if he was right on the spot after all, so close to Batang? Lobsang recalled the first part of the Karmapa's note, which of course he knew by heart:

In Tibetan lands, to the east of here.
In the region of the celestial rivers.
Opening up the landscape, the Lotus valley.

If he was right, from now on he should try and concentrate on the parallels given in the rest of the message:

My sanctuary, a shadowy cavity.
Over me sweet tears pour.
And under me, a legion of pillars.

While Lobsang speculated about the meaning hidden in those words, the outlaw got up with apparent difficulty, making a show of complaining about his foot but already moving it better, then walked away to relieve himself. On his return, he said, they could set off once again.

Kunnu watched him uneasily as he walked past, barely putting his weight on the foot he had presumably twisted in his fall. From the beginning the outlaw had seemed untrustworthy to him, but on the other hand he did not consider him a danger he needed to be especially wary of. After all, he was just a poor wretch used to making his living by small robberies. But the Mongol general made a serious error in underestimating the threat Wangchuk might pose.

The outlaw urinated genuinely, since he was so nervous he had to. He had played his cards well. His two targets were right where he wanted them. The time had come to take action.

Wangchuk turned and made a quick analysis of the situation. The Mongol had his back to him, which was perfect. He would creep up to him, then with his old blunt knife he would cut his throat like an animal chosen for sacrifice. It was crucial to eliminate the Mongol first, as he had a fearsome saber and was obviously extremely strong. Afterward he would deal with the Buddhist. Although by then he would be aware of his plan and despite his hefty build, he should pose no problem as he was totally unarmed. If Lobsang stood up to him he would stab him at the slightest opportunity, and if he tried to flee he would pursue him until he caught him. In either case, he would end up as dead as the Mongol.

Wangchuk took the first careful steps trying to make no noise. His heart began to beat furiously. Conceiving a plan inside his head was easy, but carrying it out in practice was something very different. Nevertheless, the decision was made and he would not turn back. Wangchuk held his knife tightly to give himself courage. Three yards separated him from the Mongol: if he turned at that instant he would catch him in the act, with no possible excuse to save his skin. By then he was already playing double or quits. He took one more step. A layer of cold sweat covered his forehead and back. Wangchuk was sure luck was on his side, for although the Buddhist was facing him he was deep in meditation and was keeping his eyes closed, so that he would not even see him coming. Odd sounds of birds and insects, the murmur of the river in the distance, and the whisper of the wind howling in the high peaks floated in the air. Only a yard separated him from the Mongol, who was still sitting on the rock unaware of the coming threat. Wangchuk held his breath and prepared to strike. He brandished the knife in the air, and a ray of sun filtering through the leaves of the trees gleamed on the metal.

Although Lobsang was meditating, wrapped in his own inner refuge, he had learnt to keep his mind alert. So it was that when he felt a flash of light crossing his face, he opened his eyes just in time to see the outlaw falling on Kunnu as a spider would on its prey. He did not manage to shout, but in the event there was no need. The Mongol general saw the expression of horror on Lobsang's face and, in a swift maneuver, dodged the trajectory of the knife at his throat. Kunnu's movements were faster even than Lobsang's eyes, for he always reacted a second too late: the Mongol turned quickly as he drew his sword, and the next instant he had already sunk it in the outlaw's stomach, whose incredulous gaze showed the same expression of surprise as that of Lobsang, who had been a mere witness of the event.

Kunnu had acted with such viciousness that the saber went through Wangchuk's body from one side to the other, so that the tip of the blade came out from his back dripping crimson tears. The Mongol withdrew his sword and watched the outlaw holding himself up for a few seconds. Wangchuk dropped his pathetic knife to the ground as if he could not believe what had just happened, then fell on his knees, trying in vain to stop the stream of blood issuing from his wound with the help of one hand and the stump of the other. His guts were pouring out of his stomach, as was his life. Then he felt his mouth fill with blood, which immediately began to flow from the corners of his lips.

Wangchuk writhed for a few minutes before finally dying.

Lobsang had witnessed the scene with absolute horror. Kunnu had showed incredible coolness, although he could not reproach him in any way since he had obviously acted in self-defense.

"What are we going to do with the body?" Lobsang asked when he was able to speak again.

"We'll leave it here for the carrion birds."

Lobsang nodded in silence. He was certainly not going to oppose the Mongol's wishes on that matter.

Kunnu suggested the possibility of going back to the monastery, but the abbot refused flatly. They had got too far to withdraw now when they were so close to their goal. Besides, and despite the fatal event that had just occurred, Lobsang had the certainty that he was on the right track. Kunnu agreed to his wishes.

From then on, the Mongol took the lead of the march. He was amply experienced and trained, and he would know how to cross the small valley without difficulty, even though he had never been there before. "I'll take you where you want to go," he assured Lobsang.

"I'd appreciate it," replied the abbot, whose sense of direction was not exactly his forte.

As they walked through the trees, Lobsang felt sorry for the outlaw and his stupidity. Greed had been too much for him, and not satisfied with the reward that was already his for taking them there, he had wanted all the money in the pouch, thus showing an absolute scorn for the lives of two fellow human beings. Once more, desire—the attachment to material goods—one of the three poisons of the soul, had made the wheel of samsara turn in a cycle which would go on ad infinitum.

Shortly afterward they left the trees and began to climb the mountain. Soon there was no vegetation except for a few bushes and a scattering of wilted underbrush which still clung to the dry soil. Very soon the climb began to take its toll on Lobsang, who had to stop every few steps to recover his breath. Not that he was unused to long walks, but that steep hill was torture. His legs weighed a ton, and fatigue made him choke so much his throat seized up. Kunnu avoided complaining, but his sweaty face showed that he too was having a hard time.

Twenty minutes later they had completed a quarter of the climb, and still when they looked up it seemed to them that the mountain turned a cold stare on them, as if daring them to go on climbing even though its peak was lost among the clouds of the sky.

Lobsang dropped on the ground, exhausted from the effort. He was breathing with difficulty and he could not take a single step more.

"How much further up do you need to go?" the Mongol asked scornfully. "There's nothing and nobody here, no matter how much you insist. Aren't you convinced yet?"

"Let's go on a little longer," Lobsang said as soon as he had recovered his breath.

Kunnu shrugged his shoulders and shook his head. In spite of not understanding some of the monk's decisions, deep down he admired his tenacity.

They continued their advance, slowly but steadily, thankful at least that the sun was shining that morning with a little more warmth than in recent days. The mountain was implacable, seeming to want to dissuade them from snooping around its skin, but Lobsang's heart proved to be stronger and they soon reached a considerable height.

Then, that something which Lobsang had been looking for without being able to identify suddenly appeared in front of their eyes like an oasis in the middle of the desert.

On the side of the mountain there appeared a distant black opening, as though a god had bitten a piece from it.

My sanctuary, a shadowy cavity.

And above the cave, very close, there flowed a stream whose waters ran along a quiet bed.

Over me sweet tears pour.

Lobsang looked down and saw the tops of the trees of the wood of giant cedars they had left behind them.

And under me, a legion of pillars.

Now that he had put together all the pieces of the puzzle, the message left by the Karmapa could not have been clearer.

Lobsang shook Kunnu, unable to contain his excitement. "It's here!" he cried. "It has to be."

The Mongol looked at him as if the Buddhist had lost his head as a result of the enormous effort he had made.

"Let's go in," urged Lobsang.

"All right, but we should be careful," said Kunnu. "The cave might be the lair of some wild animal." He drew his saber, still stained with the outlaw's blood, and brandished it in front of him.

The two men bent their heads and went slowly into the cave, barely lit for the first few yards by the brightness that came through the opening. At first they could not see anything except a cluster of shadows trapped in the gloom. It was not until their eyes had acclimatized to the darkness that they discovered the secret the grotto sheltered with the zeal of a first time mother.

In there was a little boy, half-naked, sitting in the lotus position, and who, surprisingly enough, appeared to be meditating. The boy opened his eyes, big and captivating, and looked at them without showing the least trace of fear or surprise, as if he had been waiting for their arrival for a long time.

Lobsang felt astonished and awed in equal parts, but more than anything else he felt tremendously happy and satisfied. It was Kunnu who, in spite of his usual aplomb and the long experience he had gained, was open-mouthed at the utterly unexpected sight which to him seemed almost supernatural.

Chögyam watched the two men who had interrupted his meditation without showing the least sign of surprise at their arrival, as his master had assured him that they would come for him before winter arrived. The tallest of the two men must be a Buddhist monk, as his appearance and clothing fit with what the hermit lama had described so often during his intense period of training. The one with the sword, on the other hand, looked like a fierce warrior, of a similar aspect to the figurines the hermit had carved in wood to beguile his leisure.

"Who are you?" asked Lobsang, breaking the silence. His voice echoed deafeningly against the walls.

"My name is Chögyam," said the boy solemnly. "And I am the one who seeks refuge in the refuge."

Lobsang, who immediately recognized those last words, threw himself full length on the floor and prostrated himself without hesitation before the true reincarnation of the Karmapa.

Seven years after his death, the tulku had finally been found.

During the journey back to the Batang Monastery, Lobsang chatted with the little boy in order to learn his story. When Chögyam told him of the tragic circumstances that had led to his falling to the bottom of the valley, it did not take long for Lobsang to piece things together: he had heard the same story before from Thupten, who had always thought his little brother had died in the fall. For the moment Lobsang felt it was more prudent not to tell Chögyam about his brother until he had passed the last test he would have to take at Tsurphu, the test which would definitely crown him as the new Karmapa. In the short term he was going to be under considerable pressure, and it would be better if he were not distracted until it was all over.

Afterward Chögyam explained how he had survived in the mountain, one of the things which most intrigued both Lobsang and Kunnu. Apparently he owed his life to an old hermit lama, recently deceased, who had found him and taken care of him from the very moment of the accident. Lobsang was not in the least surprised, since lately Buddhist monks with an ascetic vocation were legion: they were all over Tibet, and not only in the region of Ü-Tsang as had been usual up till then. At the same time he regretted not having known of his existence, particularly when he had been so close, for it was seldom that he had the chance to meet a holy man.

Halfway back it began to rain heavily, as if the sky did not approve of the arrival of Chögyam in the city, which impressed him with its grandeur and because he had never seen so many buildings together. Lobsang, astonished, observed Kunnu's generosity when he took off his own cassock and put it over Chögyam's shoulders so that he would not get soaked in the rain. Perhaps he had misjudged the general from the beginning. Although he might try to hide the fact, it was obvious that the impassive Mongol was awed by the incredible discovery of this boy.

The path leading to the monastery was already full of puddles, which they tried to avoid, while the prayer banners decorating the way were soaked and shrunken, which did not prevent the inscriptions on them from impregnating the air with their mystical blessings. The monks had run to shelter from the rain, so that there was not a soul in the immediate vicinity of the monastery... or so they thought, until at the very doorstep they made out a silhouette lying on the ground face down, which barely moved and from which issued a deep repeated lament.

When they reached him they saw that it was an old man in rags, covered in mud and dirt and practically a skeleton. The old man threw himself at Lobsang's feet and raised his emaciated face. In such a state he had trouble recognizing Lama Dechen.

He was barely audible, partly because his voice sounded broken, as if it reflected the guilt that for the last months had eaten him up within, and also because of the pattering of the sharp fall rain. Dechen, as if he were a small child, howled his head off as he pleaded for forgiveness, drowning his words in a grotesque sobbing that twisted his wrinkled face into deformity.

Lobsang could not help feel compassion for his former colleague, in spite of the many merits he had accumulated to earn such a fateful destiny. All the same, rules were rules, and once expelled he could not take him back into the monastic discipline, nor was he personally sure that would be the right thing to do.

With all the sorrow of his heart, Lobsang was about to carry on past him when Chögyam unexpectedly took Dechen by the hand and helped him to his feet, using a particular gentleness Lobsang had seldom before witnessed.

"My master in the mountain said that compassion is the quality which best and most clearly defines a good Buddhist monk," said Chögyam.

Those words, perhaps because of their simplicity, or perhaps because of the truth in them, struck Lobsang to such an extent that they made him rethink his decision.

At last, he looked at the little boy, giving him a grateful smile, then turned to the old lama, who was watching him desperately. "Dechen, I'll permit you to come back to the monastery, but you'll have to start from scratch as though you were a novice, and you can take refuge as long as you prove you're ready to wear your habit once again with honor."

That said, he helped Dechen, who could barely stand by himself, and led him inside the monastery supporting him by the shoulders. Chögyam and Kunnu went with them in silence, following the spreading fan of rain that stretched at their feet like a shining crystal walkway.

* * *

At the Tsurphu Gompa there was a different atmosphere ever since Lobsang Geshe had been entrusted with finding the tulku. The thousand or so monks who studied and lived there had joined to guarantee the success of the mission through their pujas and prayers. Kyentse Rinpoche and Tsultrim Trungpa, in particular, had no doubts about the happy result of the commission. This wave of optimism, however, was suddenly dimmed by an unexpected visitor.

A delegation from the Sakya School headed by Lama Migmar arrived at the doors of the monastery. The monks who composed it were offered accommodation and a plate of food after the long trip; nevertheless, Lama Migmar postponed the meal until after he had spoken with the abbot. It appeared that the news he was bringing could not wait, and at the same time was important enough to have made him come in person instead of sending a messenger.

Lama Migmar was led to the abbot's rooms, where Tsultrim was already expecting him with beating heart and a preoccupied look. The Sakya lama's face, in spite of the smile he tried to assume, showed deep worry. Following the usual custom with certain visits or meetings of particular significance, Lama Migmar gave Tsultrim a *khata* two yards long and the color of snow, which the abbot accepted and put around his neck. A khata was a strip of cloth, usually silk, whose length indicated the wish for a long life for whomever it was offered to, and its whiteness was a testimony to the purity in the intention of the person offering it.

At that moment Kyentse appeared. Tsultrim had summoned him so that he too could be present at the meeting. Kyentse Rinpoche bowed and greeted Lama Migmar, bringing the palms of his hands together in a sign of respect. Next came the usual exchange of courtesies.

At last Migmar spoke to explain the reason for their visit. "As you well know, given the delicate political situation Tibet has been going through since the Mongol invasion, and very specifically since the designation of Kublai as Emperor and his recent interest in Tibetan Buddhism, we at the Sakya School have been following your business closely, especially the matter of the Karmapa's succession."

"Of course," replied Tsultrim. "The future of all is at stake."

"Has there been any news recently? Has a new candidate appeared?"

Tsultrim at once brought him up to date with the situation. He told him about the finding of the note and of the trust he had placed in Lobsang Geshe to find the tulku. Very soon, he assured him, the new Karmapa would take his place on his throne in the Tsurphu Gompa.

Despite the abbot's hopeful words, Lama Migmar exhaled with resignation, very much in keeping with his anxious look. "By the time such a thing happens, it may be too late," he confided. "Our Master Drogön Chögyal Phagpa, who is at Kublai Khan's palace instructing him in the way of dharma, has sent us an urgent message. The Emperor will be traveling to Tibet in a fortnight."

"A fortnight?" Tsultrim repeated incredulously. "We'd understood he wouldn't be coming for at least a year."

"Circumstances have changed, and this opportunity came up for him," Migmar said. "He'll visit our home first, but then he'll travel here to meet the leader of the Kagyu School. And don't forget, his own possible conversion is still in the air. If this should come about, not only would it guarantee us a certain political independence, but also the certainty that the Mongols wouldn't turn violent against our people again."

Tsultrim and Kyentse exchanged puzzled looks.

"And couldn't he wait a little longer?" the abbot asked.

"An Emperor doesn't wait," replied Migmar. "He orders and disposes. And his will is done, to the letter. It's no secret that Kublai is seeking a new creed for his people. A religion which will raise the level of spirituality of his subjects and provide them with a moral code more in accord with these new times. It's for that reason that the Emperor has respected the freedom of worship within the borders of his Empire, the biggest man has ever known. All the same, the likelihood is that when Kublai embraces a new creed, he'll order that it should become the official religion of the Empire."

"It's enough for us that Buddhism should go on being the flame that illuminates Tibet," said Kyentse.

"That's exactly what's in danger," Migmar said.

"How?" Tsultrim said in alarm.

"Well, taking advantage of the existing freedom of worship, the religion of the West has arrived at our borders in the hands of the Franciscan and Dominican Orders, who have managed to extend their missionary work throughout China and Central Asia. And whether we like it or not, Christianity has also caught the Emperor's interest."

"Is that interest real?"

"Drogön Chögyal Phagpa doesn't know for sure, but that is his impression," said Migmar. "Kublai now has a westerner among his political counselors who has a certain influence over him."

That westerner was none other than Marco Polo, whom the sovereign had taken under his personal protection on meeting him. The wit of the Venetian merchant and explorer, as well as his vivid and detailed stories, had fascinated Kublai Khan, tired as he was of the apathetic reports of his civil servants.

"The Emperor is free to convert to the creed of the West if that's his final wish," Migmar concluded, "and we'll respect that. But what will happen when he declares Christianity to be the Empire's official religion? Can you imagine the consequences?"

"Do you think it could eventually mean the end of Buddhism in Tibet?" Kyentse asked.

Migmar shrugged. It was a possibility that could not be ruled out.

A heavy silence fell on the hall. The lamas avoided one another's gaze, and words refused to cross their lips. Through the window came the last sunbeam of the evening, and after it had vanished over the horizon it left the hall sunk in a pale gloom.

"For us to have a chance," said Kyentse, "Lama Lobsang wouldn't only have had to find the tulku, he'd already need to be on his way back by now."

"And do you believe that's possible?" murmured Migmar.

Kyentse shook his head. "Not even if he'd had all the luck in the world."

CHAPTER VI

Solstice

"One single day in the life of one who perceives the Sublime Truth is worth more than a hundred years of the life of one who does not perceive the Sublime Truth."

Dhammapada, 115

Since its foundation in the 11th century, the Tsurphu Monastery had not known such a time of agitation as the one currently taking place on the eve of the winter solstice. The monks' routine and their habitual peace had been thrown into disarray like a crystal vase broken into a thousand pieces. The bustle, nevertheless, was more than justified. The Kagyu lineage had never received such an illustrious visitor in all its history. No less than Kublai Khan, the almighty leader of the Mongol Empire, was a guest in its lodgings.

An army of a thousand soldiers had traveled together with the Great Khan. They had set up camp on the outskirts of Gurum, whose inhabitants could not help feeling a certain fear, even though the authorities had insisted that the visit had nothing to do with any military concerns.

Kublai felt exultant and was barely able to contain his pride. He had just emerged victorious from a long conflict with the Song dynasty in southern China, after which he had managed to occupy the whole country and reunite the Chinese government under the sole power of the Mongols. This point would mark the moment of greatest extension of the Empire, born at the beginning of the 13th century with Genghis Khan.

Along with Kublai Khan as guests at Tsurphu were his entourage of counselors, his personal guard, and Drogön Chögyal Phagpa, the Sakya lama who was doing so much for the Tibetan people. Unfortunately, the Kagyu School was still without a head, although this situation seemed to be about to change. The previous day a messenger from Batang, who had been riding day and night to the limits of his endurance, had delivered a letter which announced the finding of the tulku and his forthcoming appearance in the monastery. The letter was signed by Lobsang Geshe, but what turned out to be definitive for the Mongol emperor was that it also bore the signature of Kunnu, his efficient and loyal servant. The news was enough to make Kublai agree to wait a few more days until the arrival of the tulku, and thus to be a witness to the final test and eventual crowning of the new Karmapa.

Nevertheless, there was one counselor of Kublai's who did not share this point of view and who was defending totally opposite interests. The daring Marco Polo was leading his own crusade, whose aim was to make the Christian religion, not Buddhism, the one which would conquer the emperor's heart. It did not escape the western counselor that Kublai's conversion to the creed of his choice would mean the future conversion of the whole Empire. And Marco Polo's tenacity was also turning out to be profitable: Kublai, who had been playing a double game for some time, had recently written a letter to Pope Gregory X asking him to send a hundred missionaries to instruct him in the secrets of Christianity and evangelize the idolatrous Mongol masses.

As for Thupten, there was no denying that after several weeks at the monastery he felt extremely happy. There were so many novices at Tsurphu that he had not even been able to meet all of them, and he forgot the names of many of the ones he had met because it was impossible to learn them all. But the mere fact of finding himself surrounded by so many children had set him back on the joyful path he had known in Batang. That was the best medicine, the most effective balm for reclaiming a childhood which had been taken from him and which might have produced lifelong aftereffects if a remedy had not been found in time. Thupten had also sated his curiosity and explored every corner of the monastery. Nothing made him happier than venturing with a couple of friends along stairways and corridors usually forbidden to novices. Thupten made real efforts to adapt to the monastic discipline and was usually successful, but he could not help playing the chief part in one or other prank as a direct result of his boisterous nature. What else could be asked of the youngest novice in the whole monastery?

For his part, Kyentse Rinpoche had kept to his promise and taken care of Thupten's wellbeing, as well as his instruction and training. The relationship between them was excellent, and not a day went by without the lama devoting several hours of his time to the boy. Thupten kept close to Kyentse whenever possible, and only the emperor's arrival had prevented them from carrying on with their routine meetings during the last few days.

At last Lobsang arrived at the Tsurphu Monastery along with a delegation of monks from Batang who had escorted the tulku on his journey. Kunnu had not left Chögyam for an instant, and if necessary would have done anything to protect him. The Mongol general felt enormous satisfaction after successfully completing the mission his emperor had entrusted him with.

Neither Kyentse nor Tsultrim came out to meet them, since under no circumstances could they let the tulku see them before the final test. Therefore, it was Lama Migmar of the Sakya who had to be in charge of the welcome, together with several Kagyu lamas.

Lobsang was immediately brought up to date with the situation. Everything would be done quickly, without relaxing the usual Buddhist rigor because of it. That same evening they would celebrate the crowning of the Karmapa, once Chögyam had passed the final test, which was something everybody considered a mere detail of procedure. The preparations were under way, and no less than Kublai Khan and all his court would witness the event.

They were to take Chögyam away and keep him isolated until the moment of the ceremony.

Lobsang bent over the little boy and whispered a few words of courage. "Now we part, but we'll see each other later, at the temple. Are you nervous?"

Chögyam shook his head no. It was true. The hermit lama had prepared him thoroughly.

"The monks will take good care of you," Lobsang explained. "They'll shave your head, make you presentable, and dress you properly."

"And my brother?" Chögyam whispered. That seemed to be his only concern.

"Trust me. I'll deal with it right away."

The conversation ended. There was no time to lose. The lamas took the tulku away, and Lobsang watched him disappear round the corner of one of the monastery corridors.

As soon as the emperor learned of the tulku's arrival, Kunnu was summoned to his presence. Kublai wished to hear the tale of the facts from the general's own lips and find out whether all this story of the tulku had any truth in it.

A whole wing of the most luxurious rooms of the monastery had been reserved for the emperor and his entourage. Kunnu went to the main hall, where Kublai had ordered a provisional throne to be installed, and where he was now sitting. The emperor wore a silk tunic with gold brocade whose ampleness barely hid the excessive bulk of his body. His gaze was serene, somewhat cold at first encounter, sheltered behind a thin goatee and a carefully tended moustache in the oriental style.

Kublai was accompanied by a couple of counselors, but he took care to ensure that there was not a single Buddhist monk in the hall.

Kunnu bowed and asked permission to speak. "I don't know whether that kid is the reincarnation everybody is talking about so confidently," he declared. "But I can assure you that his finding was absolutely genuine." Kunnu then went on to give him a full account of the adventure.

The emperor, fascinated, did not miss a single detail of the story. "Has the boy been made aware of the test he has to pass so that his identity can be verified?

"He knows he has to pass some type of evaluation, but like most of us he doesn't know what it will consist of."

Kublai Khan leaned forward confidentially. "What is that boy like? Is he really something special?"

Kunnu half-closed his eyes before answering. "Well, apart from the peculiar circumstances of his finding, and the fact that he's generally sensible, in every other way he's just a little boy like any other."

The emperor seemed satisfied and dismissed Kunnu with a wave of his hand. "By the way," he said as Kunnu was leaving, "would you like to attend the ceremony?"

"I should be delighted to."

At the same time as Kunnu was answering the emperor's call, Lobsang was on his way to meet Kyentse.

The Rinpoche was in the library reading, but as soon as he glimpsed Lobsang, he made his way to him and congratulated him in a state of uncontrollable excitement. "What you did is unheard of!" he cried. "We never thought it possible that you'd find the tulku before the arrival of Kublai." Kyentse's smile filled his whole face, and his eyes shone with emotion.

"It was no big feat." Lobsang was pleased, but also a little uncomfortable with such flattery. "The Karmapa's note made it all very clear once I knew where to begin to search."

Kyentse took Lobsang by the arm and led him to a more discreet corner. His happy expression darkened suddenly, as if the curtain had been lowered in the middle of applause. Kyentse had to bring Lobsang up to date on a very delicate matter which had everyone deeply worried. "Do you know just how important the crowning of the new Karmapa is? Its significance might reach a level that until very recently would have been hard to imagine." Kyentse told Lobsang about Kublai Khan's flirting with the Christian religion, which not even all Drogön Chögyal Phagpa's powers of persuasion had been able to counteract. "According to the emperor's final decision, there'll be consequences of one kind or another for the Tibetan people," he declared.

Lobsang nodded without any apparent worry, although he was fully aware of the gravity of the situation. "How's Thupten," he asked, changing the subject and anxious to leave the political intrigues for some better moment.

"Extremely well," said Kyentse. "The ability to concentrate is not precisely his forte, but his devotion and willingness are unquestionable. He's taken to me very quickly... and the truth is I've become fond of him as well."

"Thank you, Kyentse. That boy has suffered a great deal, and he deserves all our effort. I want to make a good Buddhist monk out of him."

Kyentse asked Lobsang then to tell him in detail how he had located the tulku on the basis of the cryptic verses left by the Karmapa.

The account impressed the Rinpoche greatly. "Then Chögyam is an orphan, and he doesn't have any relatives to tell about his situation, does he?"

"Well, you know, that's just what I came to tell you about," Lobsang confessed. "In fact, the tulku has a brother."

"Really? And where is he? Who's taking care of him?"

"Well, you see... you've been doing that yourself during the last few weeks."

Kyentse frowned without understanding at first, until a few moments later the answer revealed itself. "Thupten?"

Lobsang nodded, then explained the whole story as well as the chain of coincidences brought about by fate. "The truth is that I hadn't thought of telling Chögyam about his brother until after the ceremonies, but during the journey he asked me directly whether I knew anything about where Thupten might be." Lobsang spread his arms wide, palms open. "I couldn't lie, not even for his own good."

"I understand."

"The thing is that now Chögyam is anxious to reunite with his brother. We should let them see each other so the tulku is relaxed during this evening's test. Otherwise, he won't be able to get him out of his mind."

Kyentse thought about it for a while. "You're right," he admitted. "But the meeting must be brief. Not more than five minutes."

"That will be more than enough."

Before he left, Kyentse took Lobsang's arm. His eyes revealed a certain nervousness. "Chögyam will pass the test, won't he?"

"Don't worry, Kyentse. It will be a piece of cake for the tulku."

Lobsang went to look for Thupten, finding him in a classroom of the novice school.

"Lama Lobsang!" Thupten cried as soon as he saw him at the door. "Master!" He ran and threw himself in his lap.

Lobsang swung him in the air, although straight away he put him back down on the floor with great care. "I'm very glad to see you, Thupten. But you're getting too big to pick up!"

Lobsang asked the monk in charge of the class to excuse Thupten, and he took him outside to talk in private. "Have you been happy in the Tsurphu Monastery?"

Thupten nodded repeatedly. "I think I like it better than yours," he said.

Lobsang thought that perhaps the boy associated Batang with all his negative experiences during the past year. The Tsurphu Monastery, in contrast, was somewhere far removed from his past. "Besides, I hear you're getting along very well with Kyentse."

Thupten's face shone at once. "Yes! And with Tsultrim too!"

"Ah, the abbot as well... You're going to turn out less foolish than you seemed," Lobsang said teasingly. "You're already rubbing shoulders with the bigwigs of the monastery!"

Thupten smiled broadly, and his jug ears moved at the rhythm.

"Although, don't believe I didn't miss you too," he added in his usual display of honesty.

"And so did I, Thupten," Lobsang admitted. "But now you must listen carefully. I've come to tell you some wonderful news."

Thupten looked at him expectantly, as a thousand and one possibilities crossed his mind. "I know!" he cried, "I'm going to have a new room? You see, my roommate is much older than I am and he sometimes snores like a yak. I haven't complained, you know? But sometimes I can't get a wink of sleep."

Lobsang held back his laughter. "No, it's much more important than that," he said more seriously. "It's about your brother Chögyam."

Thupten's cheerful expression darkened as though the sun had been covered by a black cloud.

Lobsang crouched to the same level as the boy. "Calm down, Thupten. I told you it was good news. Your brother is alive."

Thupten took a step back, as if Lobsang's words had slapped him in the face. An incredulous look appeared in his eyes, where tears were welling up. "But master, that can't be true. I saw him fall off the cliff myself."

"It's true, Thupten. And it's also true that he survived the fall."

"Really?" Hope glimmered in his eyes.

"I would never lie to you. Least of all about a matter like this."

Thupten's expression showed that he was still not at all sure.

"Would you like to see him? He's right here. In the monastery."

166

Thupten's mouth opened in an almost perfect circle. "Yes! Please!"

"All right," Lobsang said. "But you can only be with him for a couple of minutes."

"Why?"

"Chögyam is special. He's a very important little boy."

"I don't understand. Chögyam is my brother. What makes him so special?"

Lobsang put his hands on Thupten's shoulders and addressed him with utmost solemnity. "It's hard to explain. But there's something you must understand very clearly. At this moment, Chögyam is the hope of Tibet."

They had moved Chögyam to a tiny alcove where a monk was busy making him look presentable for the ceremony. The place was as dimly lit as almost all the rooms of the monastery. Those surroundings, with their shrouding of shadow and misty light, contributed to meditation and helped the soul to relax fully.

Lobsang stepped inside and asked the monk to leave them for a moment so that the tulku could receive an exceptional visitor. "It'll only be a moment," he assured him.

The monk did as he was asked, and Lobsang gestured to Thupten to come into the room. "I'll wait outside."

Thupten was trembling. Deep down he still could not believe that Chögyam was alive, and until he could confirm the fact with his own eyes he would not truly believe it. The door which barred him from finding out seemed to him at that moment like an impenetrable wall he did not see himself as capable of crossing. An unjustified feeling of guilt for not having taken care of him as he should have, being the elder, made him a little afraid of meeting his brother again. Lobsang patted him on the back and gave him the trace of a push, which helped him to recover his self-control. Then Thupten took the definitive step. He walked into the room and closed the door after him.

When the two brothers looked at each other it took them a few seconds to react. It had been a full year since their separation and they had both grown, although in proportion, so that Thupten was still a head taller than Chögyam. Otherwise they had changed little and their faces were perfectly recognizable. Their eyes were riveted on each other. Thupten's lower lip was quivering, and in his eyes tears of emotion were welling up and about to run down his cheeks. Deep down inside he felt a part of himself coming together which he had believed lost forever, as if a light shone again in that corner of his soul that had been sunk in darkness. Chögyam too tried to suppress the urge to cry that was coming up his throat and formed a knot round his vocal chords. His heart was beating hard and he was overwhelmed by a joy for which there were no words, and which he would never again in his life experience so intensely. When at last they were able to come out of their paralysis, they threw themselves at each other and fused together in an embrace which in an instant returned to them the wellspring of feelings that had been lost since the fateful storm.

"When you fell into the ravine after mom and dad, I thought the three of you were dead." Thupten was crying and laughing at the same time. The mere mention of their parents was enough to heighten the emotion of that moment. "If I'd known you had survived, I'd have done anything to find you."

"There was no way you could know," replied Chögyam, rather more serenely, "so don't worry about that. What's important is that we're both well."

Thupten nodded vehemently, without letting go of Chögyam's arms, as if he felt he was going to lose him again.

"I never stopped thinking about you all this time," Chögyam said. He had been able to calm the whirlwind of emotions he felt bubbling inside him more quickly than his brother. "What happened to you? Did you reach Batang and the Buddhist monks took you into their monastery?"

Thupten confirmed this, although it was not the whole truth. He would have the chance to tell him about his period with the outlaw some other time. "And how did you get to safety?"

"Thanks to a hermit who lived in the mountain. He rescued me and took care of me till the day he died. He was a prodigious lama who taught me everything I know about the Buddha and his teachings."

"So you want to be a Buddhist monk too?"

"I'm going to be the best of the lamas," Chögyam said with absolute conviction.

Thupten was not surprised. His brother had always shown clear signs of intelligence. "You'll have to study a lot for that. And you'll need a good teacher to take you as a disciple," Thupten warned him. "My teacher is Lobsang!" he said proudly.

"I like Lobsang," Chögyam said. "He's wise and just. And during the long journey to Gurum he passed on some teachings to me."

Thupten took on a thoughtful pose. "Lobsang doesn't take personal disciples, you know? I'm an exception. Although if I spoke to him, I might be able to convince him." Thupten did not stop his train of thought there. "Or if not.., I know who'd be perfect for you! Kyentse!"

"I don't know him."

"You don't? Well, in many ways he's very much like Lobsang. Well, Kyentse isn't as big as my master, of course. What I mean is that they're both very understanding and patient, and experts in the teachings of the Buddha. Take a good look if you see him; you'll recognize him because the bones of his face stand out and his eyebrows are very close together." Thupten had gotten into his stride and there was no way anyone could stop him turning back into the chatterbox he had always been. "You know who else could be your teacher? Tsultrim, the abbot of the monastery. He's very fat." He laughed. "Sometimes he gets angry, and then it looks as if his frog's eyes are going to pop out of his face." Chögyam joined in his brother's laughter. "But he's also an excellent lama."

There was a brief silence, and the brothers looked at each other, smiling.

"Why do they say you're special?" Thupten asked with real interest.

Chögyam already had a pretty good idea. During the journey he had heard the monks talking about the tulku and his particular significance. But he chose to keep quiet because he would not have known how to explain it. "That's what they all say, but I'm not very sure."

At that moment Lobsang came into the room. Time was up. The visit had seemed extremely short to them.

Lobsang urged them to say their farewells and took Thupten's hand to take him away.

"I want one like his!" he cried as they crossed the threshold.

Chögyam looked at him in puzzlement.

"A black hat just like the one you're wearing on your head!" he heard Thupten say just as he left the room, although there was nothing covering his head.

Everything was ready for the ceremony.

First the final test would take place, and immediately afterward the crowning of the new Karmapa. In fact, this procedure was not the usual one. Under normal circumstances the test should have taken place more time in advance, so as to establish the candidate's authenticity beyond doubt. Strictly speaking, Chögyam was still a candidate until he passed the test, in spite of the firm evidence which pointed to him unequivocally as the true reincarnation of the Karmapa. However, Kublai's presence had upset everything, and both ceremonies would take place consecutively, without any pause in between.

The stage for an event of such magnitude could be none other than the main temple at Tsurphu.

In front of the altar an empty space had been cleared close to the throne of the Karmapa, at the feet of which a thick woolen carpet had been spread, with geometric and floral motifs that indicated the place reserved for Chögyam. Facing it, sitting on soft cushions in the front row, were the most illustrious figures present: Kublai Khan, escorted by four of his most influential counselors (among them Marco Polo), and Drogön Chögyal Phagpa, leader of the Sakya School and the one in charge of directing the ceremony. Behind them innumerable rows of Buddhist monks, some of whom had arrived from Lhasa for the occasion, crowded the temple so that there was not a single space left free. In addition, on one side of the throne, in a privileged position, was a full representation of the most select lamas, notably among them Lobsang and Lama Migmar, and on the other side a large group of novices chosen from among the most outstanding of the monastery. Lobsang had intervened so that there would also be a place for Thupten, who more than anyone else deserved to witness the historic crowning of his younger brother.

A mantra initiated by Drogön Chögyal Phagpa was the starting point for the ceremony. All the attendants, except the Mongols and the sole westerner present, came together in one voice, filling the hall with a resonance that penetrated the walls of the mind. Marco Polo was not very optimistic, but he was still hopeful that something would not go according to plan and that somehow the whole ceremony would be a failure. Otherwise Kublai would most likely convert to Buddhism long before the arrival of the hundred missionaries requested from the Pope.

The Sakya leader ceased the opening chant, and the Buddhist temple was once again filled with the deep, vibrant silence so characteristic of the Buddhist sanctuaries. Then he gave a sign and Chögyam, who had been waiting in an adjacent room, appeared on the stage led by a monk who showed him where he should stand. After this the monk left the boy in front of the crowd and went out the way he had come.

Chögyam, with his head already shaved and wearing a saffron robe, walked slowly, carefully taking note of everything going on around him. The altar stood against the wall, cluttered with the usual offerings—bowls filled with water, tormas, and sacred texts wrapped in cloth—and an imposing Buddha on the central shelf, seated on a lotus flower with a subtle smile and exaggeratedly long earlobes. The memory of the modest altar in the cave came to Chögyam's mind. It had been nothing more than a ledge of rock on which stood a simple bowl and a wooden Buddha carved by the hermit himself. The essence, he thought, was still the same.

Chögyam walked past the Karmapa's throne, which had not been occupied since the death of his predecessor, and as he had been instructed to, bowed to the authorities in front of him as he had been instructed to. That was one of the few precise instructions he had been given. As for the rest, he had been told to act naturally and to follow the guidelines the lama in charge of the ceremony would be giving him. Chögyam sat on the rug with his legs crossed, so far showing an extraordinary serenity.

Chögyam felt the atmosphere of the place to be very charged, which was not surprising given the amount of people present in the temple. The greasy smell of the lamps of yak butter mingled with the scent of incense, without either smell prevailing over the other. Before him a man dressed in fine clothes, with a goatee beard, stood out dramatically from the rest. He was studying him with curiosity in his eyes and a haughtiness which could easily be forgiven in the most powerful ruler on Earth. This must be the Great Khan, to whom he had to show the utmost respect, according to what he had been told. But even more than the emperor himself, Chögyam's attention was caught by another individual with white skin and a prominent nose, together with many other traits very different from the usual Asian type. Moreover, this foreigner was the only person who was looking at him with a certain distrust, as opposed to the Buddhists, whose gaze expressed nothing but the deepest veneration.

Chögyam turned to the right and quickly made out Lobsang, accompanied by a group of much older lamas. His close proximity immediately comforted his heart. But his joy was even greater when to his left, surrounded by a group of novices, he saw Thupten smiling with pride and whispering to all around him that this was his brother.

Hundreds of eyes were fixed on him, but Chögyam was not nervous. What was this compared to having spent whole mornings learning to meditate on the edge of a rock shelf high up on a mountain side, feeling the freezing breeze winding its slippery way among the peaks of the range? His master, the hermit monk, had prepared him well.

Drogön Chögyal Phagpa then began an amiable conversation with Chögyam, asking him simple questions about himself, such as his name, his age, or where he had been born. As he answered these questions, several monks paraded behind Chögyam and waited in silence near the altar, behind the boy. Next, the Sakya leader began to declaim a solemn speech listing the Karmapa's virtues and praising his incomparable work for the benefit of all sentient creatures. At last he revealed what for Chögyam was an open secret and the real reason why the Buddhists considered him such a special boy.

"You are the tulku, the Karmapa reincarnated and as such you'll be in charge of keeping the Buddha's torch of dharma alive. And for everyone to know and to dispel any trace of doubt about your identity, you will submit to the tests I shall now give you." Drogön Chögyal Phagpa pointed to the monks who had just come in. "Turn around and greet Kyentse, your most beloved disciple, joyfully. And Tsultrim, the pertinacious abbot of this monastery, whom we had kept hidden from your presence until now."

Chögyam turned to take a closer look at seven monks who had fanned out behind him without his noticing. They all wore identical habits, and no external sign on their clothing differentiated them from one another. Their faces, moreover, were serious and expressionless, with the clear aim of avoiding any revealing emotion. Chögyam swept his glance over them all. He did not know any of them. What was worse, he did not recognize them either!, which presumably he ought to in some way.

Chögyam looked back and saw the eyes of the Mongol emperor fixed on his, following the unfolding of the test with great attention. By now he did not need anybody to tell him that he must not fail, since if he did, there would be important consequences. Chögyam remained calm, and put his mind to work. Luck, at least, was on his side. Barely a few hours earlier Thupten had briefly described the two lamas he had to identify.

Singling out Tsultrim would pose no difficulty. Only one of the seven monks was obese, and if that were not enough, he could confirm his guess by noting his enormous protruding eyes. Chögyam took the abbot's hand in his own and spoke his name loudly and clearly, so that those in the first row could hear him. The tension in Tsultrim's face relaxed. He prostrated himself immediately before the tulku and then turned to the group of lamas on his right, between Lobsang and Migmar.

Guessing Kyentse's identity, on the other hand, was going to be a more difficult challenge. Four of the remaining monks had angular features. And of these four, three boasted eyebrows prominent enough to confuse Chögyam. In short, he had one chance out of three of guessing correctly.

Marco Polo realized at once that the boy was hesitating over his choice, and a perverse grin flickered at the corner of his mouth. Perhaps, after all, the test would not be a mere formality for the tulku, as he had always thought. The Buddhists, strangely, were behaving with the greatest rigor, with no fear that their excessive zeal might turn against them.

Chögyam could spin things out no longer, so that he finally pointed to one of the lamas, at least trying to make it appear that he was doing so with absolute conviction.

Kyentse, swelling with pride, broke into a smile which filled his whole face. "Master, I'm glad to see you again," he said, immensely happy.

Chögyam nodded and let out a small sigh of relief. He had chosen him because of the three he was the one whose eyes shone brightest.

Meanwhile a growing concern began to trouble Lobsang. After watching the scene very carefully, his critical eye told him something was not right, even though the result indicated just the opposite. Kyentse and Tsultrim were too involved and immersed in the ceremony to think clearly, but from Lobsang's point of view, the tulku had not acted in the way he would have expected. Chögyam should have recognized them much more naturally, not analytically, even coldly, like this.

Drogön Chögyal Phagpa now beckoned Chögyam to sit down on the carpet once again. He asked him not to move from his place while he and other lamas left for a few minutes to conclude a series of enormously important preparations.

The final test had not yet ended and in fact was going to get even more complicated.

The Sakya leader and the Mongol emperor directed their steps to a nearby hall where ritual objects and other utensils of the sort were kept. Kyentse and Tsultrim joined them and disappeared behind the door. To make the wait more pleasant, the musician monks at the back of the temple began to play a symphony, and a choir of cavernous voices joined in the spirited music. Chögyam had by now lost some of his calm. He could not help but feel the tickle of nerves running up and down his legs like a parade of spiders.

Lobsang debated with himself whether to say something about the doubts that were stirring in him. He was surely making a mountain out of a molehill, but he had better make sure in case some piece of the puzzle had not been put in its proper place. Lobsang walked toward the hall where the others had gathered and went in, even though his presence was not expected.

As soon as he walked in, he noticed that not only was he not told off for his audacity, but he was welcomed gladly. The discoverer of the tulku could most certainly witness the preparations for the test.

Lobsang saw Drogön Chögyal Phagpa and Tsultrim Trungpa carefully placing a series of objects on a tray. He stretched his neck to see. The objects were nothing but ghaus.

"What happens next?" Kublai Khan asked, frankly intrigued.

"Only one of these holy pendants belonged to the late Karmapa," Drogön Chögyal Phagpa explained. "Now Chögyam will have to choose one of them following the dictates of his spirit. If he really is the tulku, as we all believe, he won't make any error in his choice."

Next they took a bigger tray, on which they began to place a selected variety of musical instruments. Lobsang recognized a kangling, cymbals, and a conch.

"In this case," the Sakya leader explained, "Chögyam will have to point out the Karmapa's favorite instrument."

Lobsang, harboring a terrible premonition, bent over Kyentse.

"Which was his favorite instrument?" he whispered in his ear.

"The conch, of course," Kyentse whispered back. "The Karmapa learned to play in the last stage of his life and became a true virtuoso. It's a very complicated instrument to play, did you know that? You must master the technique of continuous breathing."

Lobsang paled all of a sudden, and for an instant he felt he was short of air. How could he have been so blind despite having had the evidence right in front of him all this time? He now realized, much to his chagrin, that he had made a terrible mistake which might have catastrophic consequences.

Obviously… the tulku was Thupten… and not Chögyam, as he had always believed.

The signs had been there for whomever knew how to read them, but he had not even taken them into account. Now, with all the cards on the table, at last he had a whole vision of the truth.

The key of the conch had opened his eyes and made him understand, but there were many other things he had not seen in time.

Lobsang remembered Thupten's reaction the first time he saw Kyentse: the way he spontaneously threw himself into his arms, full of enthusiasm, in spite of the initial distrust he usually felt toward adults as a result of the time he had spent with the outlaw.

Lobsang also remembered Thupten's first visit to the Batang Temple. And specifically, even more than the keen interest he had shown in everything, the naturalness with which he had climbed onto the throne, as if he had been doing it all his life.

Above all he remembered what he had said as they crossed the mountain pass that had taken his family's lives: *I was falling and my brother was safe, you know? But at the last moment, a gust of wind changed everything. It really should have been me, not Chögyam, the one to fall to the bottom of that valley.*

Lobsang was now sure he was not mistaken, and that a whimsical gust of wind had crossed the path that destiny had reserved for Thupten. The problem was that his discovery had come too late.

Thoughts were crowding inside Lobsang's head. He knew everything that was at stake, but there was no way he could share that unsettling revelation with the others. Or at least not at that moment, nor in the middle of the ceremony. How could he tell them that the tulku was not Chögyam but another boy? They would fall into disrepute. It would sow the seed of distrust in the emperor, who would doubt the solemnity of the ceremony and the rigor of the Kagyu School, and by extension, of Buddhism as a whole.

Lobsang realized at once that it did not really matter what he did. As soon as Chögyam failed the test, the effect it would have on Kublai would be the same: distrust toward the Buddhist religion would immediately take root in the Great Khan's heart, and all Drogön Chögyal Phagpa's efforts would have been in vain.

There was still the possibility, of course, that Chögyam would pass the test by himself if luck stayed with him. In fact, that was clearly the only way they could come out unscathed from the mess they had gotten themselves into without either failing in their principles or disappointing the emperor.

Lobsang had no false illusions about this. Chögyam would have to choose between the three ghaus, and if he was right, the same procedure would be repeated with the musical instruments. His chances of success were limited, but not necessarily remote. Somehow, whether by good fortune or intuition, Chögyam had already hit the mark with the identities of Kyentse and Tsultrim:

although perhaps precisely because of that, Lobsang thought, the boy might have used up his ration of good luck for the day.

Lobsang decided that if fate allowed Chögyam to succeed in the test, he would wait for the emperor's definitive departure before clarifying the matter. Then he would explain to the others the reason for the confusion, and as soon as Thupten was proved to be the authentic tulku, they would sort things out and restore everything to its proper place again.

At that moment Marco Polo came into the hall, and Lobsang left aside his thoughts to return to reality. The emperor's counselor had not been invited, so straight away he earned the hostile looks of the four lamas present. All the same, Kublai summoned him with a wave of his hand, and Drogön Chögyal Phagpa, who was about to show his opposition, had to bite his tongue.

The impression Lobsang had of Marco Polo was not a particularly good one. His haughty attitude and suspicious expression during the ceremony made it very clear that the Buddhist creed did not deserve his respect. On the other hand, Lobsang understood the Venetian's position. Indoctrinated by Christianity, in a cultural and social frame diametrically opposed to Lobsang's, it was logical that he should defend the interests of the western world. Lobsang could not blame him for that. He would have probably done the same in his place.

Kublai spoke with Marco Polo and explained what was involved in the second part of the test. The counselor frowned as he looked at the objects on the trays. Next he raised his eyebrows and whispered something in the emperor's ear. Kublai half-closed his eyes, adopted a meditative pose, and nodded as if in agreement.

"Aren't three objects too few?" he asked. Of course it was a rhetorical question. Usually, nobody contradicted the emperor.

"It's the tradition," the Sakya leader said, as amiably as he could.

"Yes, but if there were seven of them, then we could discard the factor of chance almost entirely."

The lamas looked at each other in confusion, unsure how to react.

"It won't be a problem," Tsultrim said at last. "The real tulku could identify his personal objects among a hundred if necessary."

"Of course," Kyentse added, "the tulku still retains the memory of his previous life in his spirit's essence."

"Excellent," said the emperor approvingly. "Then let it be seven pendants on the tray."

Marco Polo, profoundly satisfied, licked his lips with relish. The boy had already hesitated during the first part of the test, so the more difficult they made things for him the better. With luck his nerves would end up betraying him.

Lobsang, who had not opened his mouth, felt a cold sweat spreading across his back and hands. His last hope had vanished into thin air by the emperor's express wish.

Shortly afterward they all returned to the main hall of the temple and once again took their places. Kyentse himself, convinced he was dealing with his old master, was in charge of placing the tray at Chögyam's feet with almost infinite devotion. A pious silence filled the hall once more, and without further delay Drogön Chögyal Phagpa resumed the ceremony.

The Sakya leader turned to Chögyam with soft words, asking him to choose among the seven pendants resting on the tray. He did not specify anything else, nor was he expected to. Chögyam knew that choosing was easy, the difficulty lay in being correct, and that and no other was the test's true secret. The problem was that although each of the pendants had its own characteristics, to Chögyam's eyes they all looked alike, and to all intents and purposes none of the ghaus called his attention any more than the others.

The minutes went by and Chögyam could not decide, however much he mulled over it. The tulku no longer gave any impression of self-assurance and many monks were beginning to fidget, restless at the uncertain outcome of the ceremony. Chögyam's hands were shaking, and his pulse had increased considerably. The future of a nation rested on the shoulders of a little boy of six, who by now was fully aware that what was expected of him and what he could deliver were two very different realities. Chögyam, unable to bear the pressure any longer, was about to break down.

Lobsang had lowered his head, not daring to look up. The boy was suffering because he wanted to pass the test, even though it was obvious that it was not within his reach. Lobsang in turn was tormented inside. His had been the responsibility of finding the tulku, and his had been the mistake. He only wished that the nightmare would end as soon as possible. There would be time later to analyze what had happened and face up to the consequences.

From where he was standing Thupten did not have a good view of the pendants on the tray, but even so, he would not have hesitated for a moment over which one to choose. It was strange, because although it was the first time he had seen that beautiful ghau, deep down he had the impression of recognizing it, as if he had had the chance to see it before. Even more than that, this inexplicable sensation, far from going away, intensified as the minutes passed, to the point where Thupten had convinced himself that the ghau was his and had always been his.

Thupten felt frustrated at the impossibility of helping his brother without being discovered. In the middle of that sepulchral silence, even if he had only whispered, his voice would have echoed from each and every one of the temple's walls. And if he opted for gesturing, not a second would have passed before a hundred eyes caught him pointing where he had no business to. Much to his chagrin, and unless something came up at the last minute, everything indicated that Chögyam would have to do everything by himself.

Chögyam raised his eyes to see that all the monks were looking at him now with their souls crushed, all vestiges of veneration gone from their eyes. His insecurity when it came to choosing the ghau, as well as his growing nervousness, clearly visible to all, had taken away much of the regard he had earned. Chögyam had no choice but to pick a pendant at random, but he was not ready to accept that nerves, rather than serenity, would be the main emotion guiding him in his final choice. Surely the hermit, his dear master of the mountain, would approve.

To begin with, Chögyam closed his eyes. Then he crossed his legs, putting each foot on the opposite thigh and his cupped hands on his knees. Then he began to hum lightly, showing clearly that he was reciting a mantra.

A wave of puzzlement ran through the temple from one end to the other. They had never seen anything like this before.

"What is he doing?" whispered Marco Polo.

179

"He's adopted the lotus position, and he's going to meditate," Kublai himself explained. He was as perplexed as everyone else.

Marco Polo had thought Chögyam was cornered, but he had not expected that turn in the events at all, and it made him wary. The boy was as cunning as the devil and if he was really planning something and not simply gaining time, he could not think what it could be.

Chögyam fixed his attention on a single spot inside his head. He isolated each one of his emotions, especially those that were keeping him tense, and quieted his mind, guided by the sound of his own voice.

The process went on for more than five minutes, during which the audience waited on edge, holding their breath for a long time.

By the time Chögyam opened his eyes again, he had regained his calm. The trembling stopped and the beating of his heart went back to normal. Chögyam looked up and stared at the emperor, who was beginning to show signs of impatience. He turned his head to the right, where the faces of Kyentse and Tsultrim no longer showed the exultation that had been visible up to the final stage of the ceremony. Lobsang for his part gave him the trace of a smile, as if telling him not to worry even if he failed the test. Finally Chögyam twisted his head round to the left, where his large eyes met Thupten's. To his surprise it was now his brother who wore the black crown which nobody else could see and which, without realizing, he himself had brought back with him from the heart of the mountain. Once again the hat had changed wearers.

For a few moments both of them stared fixedly at one another, until Thupten blinked.

That was enough for them to understand each other.

To Chögyam the blink had not seemed natural, and immediately, stifling a smile, he thought that after a year his older brother had still not learned to wink. Chögyam had understood the message, and although he did not know what Thupten might have to offer to enable him to solve the test, the black crown made him trust him completely.

Thupten was not sure whether Chögyam had caught the sign, but he soon saw that his brother had not forgotten the trick they had planned together to always guess correctly which hand their mother was hiding the piece of cake in. The mechanics would not change in this case, and the only difference would be that the trick would fool not their mother but the sovereign of the most powerful empire on the planet.

A single glance was enough to conceive the plan. Now they had to carry it out. Chögyam put his hands over the first ghau and held them very close, inches away from it, as if he were sensing the energy of the object. Next Chögyam looked out of the corner of his eye toward Thupten, who remained impassive. The first pendant was ruled out.

The operation was repeated three times more until they reached the fourth ghau on the tray. This time Thupten blinked hard, leaving no room for doubt. Chögyam did not think twice. He picked up that ghau and hung it round his neck, keeping an eye on the audience to see if he was right.

Drogön Chögyal Phagpa sighed in relief and felt that once again he was back in tune with the ceremony. Lobsang was left gaping in astonishment, unable to find any explanation for the incredible streak of luck Chögyam was having. Kyentse and Tsultrim recovered the faith in the tulku they had nearly lost after the last heart-throbbing minutes. Emperor Kublai showed signs of surprise, and Marco Polo put his hands to his head in frustration at Chögyam's unqualified success.

The test went on as planned, with the story repeating itself when Chögyam had to choose among the different musical instruments on a bigger tray. The tulku was confirmed, and there followed his coronation before the fervent eyes of all present, including the emperor himself, whose heart turned notably toward the Buddhist creed from that day on. When the ceremony ended Chögyam took the throne of the Karmapa, which had remained empty for the previous seven years.

Chögyam's short-lived appointment as the new head of the Kagyu School lasted less than forty-eight hours.

As soon as the ceremony was over and Lobsang was able to speak with the two brothers alone, they confessed what had happened, without glossing over any details. Lobsang was not so much surprised by the story as by the audacity shown by the two boys at such a critical moment. Lobsang asked them to keep the secret, and it was not until the emperor was far enough away that Lobsang revealed the true identity of the tulku to the Kagyu lamas.

Everything became clear once Lobsang had revealed the full details. There was great amazement since the whole business was so exceptional, but they all accepted the evidence which the facts dictated. Lobsang was congratulated for his quick thinking and for managing the crisis in such an efficient and exemplary manner. Thupten, of course, was subjected to a new test, which he passed without the slightest difficulty, showing beyond any doubt his status as the reincarnated Karmapa.

Later on came his coronation, which this time proved to be the definitive one.

EPILOGUE

Thupten turned out to be one of the most outstanding Karmapas of his time.

Instructed by Kyentse Rinpoche himself, he received the complete transmission of the Kagyu tradition, which he was able to assimilate in record time. From his earliest years he built bridges with the rest of the Buddhist schools in order to unify doctrines and currents of thought. He was also a great traveler, who preached ceaselessly throughout Tibet, China, and Mongolia. Conscientious and multidisciplinary, in his adult age he became a sage, and some of the most remarkable texts that would rule the future of Tibetan Buddhism came from his hand. Before he died, and following his predecessor's example, Thupten left a note with precise instructions for locating his own successor.

Chögyam also received instruction at the Tsurphu Monastery and became a lama, thus fulfilling his childhood dream. Also, following Lobsang's footsteps, he reached the level of Geshe very early in life. Chögyam never left his brother's side and became his most faithful disciple. He went with him on his travels, organizing the celebration of his massively attended ceremonies, and even collaborated closely in the writing of the famous monastic texts. Chögyam crowned his career in the best possible way by proudly taking on the position of abbot of the Tsurphu Gompa.

Lobsang returned to Batang a few days after the confirmation of Thupten as Karmapa, even though it saddened him greatly to leave the boys. But Lobsang was firmly committed to his beloved monastery, his missionary work, and his unconditional support for the bhikkhuni. Only when he reached old age did he leave the region of Kham behind forever and fulfill his old dream of returning to the Tsurphu Monastery, where he spent the last years of his life devoted to meditation. Shortly before his death, Lobsang entered tukdam, the crystalline light of the final meditation, in which he remained until he breathed his last. His body was wrapped in a cloth and watched over in a small room for three days by monks and lamas. However, on the fourth day, when they came to take away his body for the obsequies, on taking away the cloth they found nothing except nails and hair. In addition, many were the monks during that interlude who reported seeing strange luminous phenomena around the monastery.

The Karmapa didn't hesitate for a moment to have a stupa erected in honor of Lobsang, the most faithful of Buddhists, who had been able to reach Enlightenment without setting out to.

AUTHOR'S NOTE

Marco Polo served Kublai Khan for seventeen years, during which he became a member of his diplomatic corps and even ruled over the Chinese city of Yangzhou for three years. After a quarter of a century in faraway lands, Marco Polo returned to Venice in 1295. His family did not recognize him at first, having thought him dead long before.

Pope Gregory X, in what is considered one of the Church's worst strategic errors, did not take the Mongol emperor's request seriously enough. Apart from a letter and some gifts, instead of a hundred missionaries he sent only two Dominican friars, who decided to return halfway through their journey, frightened by the innumerable dangers they encountered.

Kublai Khan was the first Mongol emperor to convert to Buddhism. This was a crucial event for Tibet, and its main consequence was the transfer of Mongol power to a Tibetan citizen. The chosen one was none other than Drogön Chögyal Phagpa, spiritual mentor to Kublai Khan, who took on the regency of the country and the authority over his own people.

The Sakya lineage ruled the policy of Tibet until the mid-14th century. Afterward, different secular dynasties succeeded one another in power, until in the 16th century the Gelug School, led by the lineage of the Dalai Lama, took over the government of the Tibetan people.

The Mongol governor Altan Khan, Kublai's grandson, also converted to Tibetan Buddhism, declaring it the official religion of the Empire. This action favored its expansion through all the territories under his command.

At present, Buddhism is the fourth religion in the world by number of followers, and the Dalai Lama continues to be the ruler of the Tibetan government in exile after the invasion of the country in 1950 by the Chinese army.

The figure of the Karmapa has lived on to the present day, still being considered one of the most revered spiritual leaders of

Tibetan Buddhism. Today the seventeenth reincarnation of the Karmapa continues to devote himself to meditation, to living the principles of wisdom and compassion in full, and to spreading the teachings of the Buddha throughout the globe.

The Karmapa is known as the bearer of the Black Crown.

Legend has it that a hundred thousand dakinis wove this crown from their own hair and that they offered it to the Karmapa because of his high level of self-realization. It is also said that the true crown, not the replica normally used in the ceremonies, does not have a physical reality but a spiritual one, and that all the Karmapas in history have worn it always and at all times, even though no one can see it except those whose hearts are pervaded with purity.

AFTERWORD

Dear reader,

I hope you have enjoyed this novel. And if it is so I would appreciate your commentary to Amazon so that other readers may know and share your evaluation. This is very important in order to be able to continue offering my work at such a reasonable price. It will only take you a minute of your time.

Thank you for reading!

Contact email: josevicentealfaro@outlook.com

Made in the USA
Middletown, DE
18 August 2022

71685000R00113